Praise for Beth Williamson's *The Tribute*

5 Roses "'Wow', I have not read the other books in this series, but oh my "God" this book rocked. I couldn't put it down and now I am running to get the other ones when I can for sure."

~ *Nicole, My Book Cravings*

4 Spurs "The Tribute has plenty of action, of all types, to keep you turning the pages and all the characters, even the secondary characters like ex-gunslinger Kincaid, do their part to keep it interesting. This is a fast, sexy, read. Guaranteed to please!"

~ *Carol, Love Western Romances*

5 Blue Ribbons "Beth Williamson thrills her readers with this newest installment in her MALLOY FAMILY series. There's no shortage of wonderful characters who will draw readers into the storyline and keep you eagerly reading."

~ *Chrissy Dionne, Romance Junkies*

5 Angels and Recommended Read "Oh my goodness, Beth Williamson has done it again with another remarkable Malloy story... Great job, Beth Williamson, for this is one Malloy worth waiting for! I'm now anxious to get Book 7, Noah's Story."

~ *Lena C., Fallen Angels Reviews*

5 Hearts "Ms. Williamson has done an extraordinary job of telling this story with a myriad of problems to be encountered. The problems of hired guns, murder, manipulation and unrequited love are just some of the tribulations. I was intrigued with this nail-biting story and could not put it down. It is an exhilarating look at the Old West and I recommend it highly!"

~ *Brenda Talley, The Romance Studio*

"...Full of love, life, and family, The Tribute was everything I wanted it to be and more. It is truly one of the best western historical novels I have read this year. Beth Williamson continues to be one of my favorite writers and I am happy to note that there is yet another installment to this spectacular series."

~ *Talia Ricci, Joyfully Reviewed*

4 Cups "The Tribute is a lovely page-turner. The storytelling creates more than simple visualizations; the reader is pulled into a living, breathing world drawn by Williamson's vivid words...This is one passionate tale that should be owned."

~ *Cherokee, Coffee Time Romance*

The Tribute

Beth Williamson

A Samhain Publishing, Ltd. publication.

Samhain Publishing, Ltd.
512 Forest Lake Drive
Warner Robins, GA 31093
www.samhainpublishing.com

The Tribute
Copyright © 2007 by Beth Williamson
Print ISBN: 1-59998-647-7
Digital ISBN: 1-59998-447-4

Editing by Sasha Knight
Cover by Scott Carpenter

First Samhain Publishing, Ltd. electronic publication: March 2007
First Samhain Publishing, Ltd. print publication: December 2007

Dedication

To my good friend and critique partner, Sasha. Thank you for your friendship, support, guidance, and everything in between. Lotsa love, babe.

Prologue

April 1888

The sun warmed the chilly morning and Brett held his hat dutifully as a breeze blew through the small cemetery. The sound of cicadas and crickets played a requiem for Martin Samson. Finally, Brett's wait was over.

He never expected a pair of deuces would win him a ranch in a poker game. He still couldn't believe the codger had thrown the deed into the pot. The whole thing started at the regular Saturday night game in the saloon in Cheshire, not some high-stakes game. He'd known Martin Samson all his life. Strange old bird who kept to himself. Raised a few cattle on his ranch and came into town for supplies now and then.

Now he'd passed on and Brett was making good on his promise made almost a year ago.

"Why the hell did you put that in the pot?" Brett had asked as he perused the deed.

Martin shrugged. "I ain't got nobody to leave it to. Doc says I ain't got but a few months to live. Might just as well make sure somebody gets it that's gonna take care of it. If there's one thing I know about you Malloy boys, you take care of your own."

Brett had stared at the paper in his hands. His. A ranch. All his. The paper trembled just slightly in his grip so he folded it and set it on the scarred table top.

"I'll tell you what. I'm not gonna insult you by trying to give it back, but I ain't gonna take it from you now. You can live there, do whatever you been doing until you're gone. I'll take care of speaking some words over your grave and make sure you get a proper burial."

Martin nodded. "That sounds right fair, Brett Malloy. And I sure do appreciate it."

Brett shook Martin's gnarled hand, surprised to find the older man's grip weak, his hands bony and slender. Whatever illness he had was definitely sucking the life out of him.

Out of respect for Martin, Brett stayed away from the ranch. He tucked that deed down deep in his stash of private things at home and waited. One thing Brett was good at was waiting.

Brett kept the knowledge that he had his own property, his own ranch, to himself. Surprisingly he hadn't told his brother Trevor, even though he was closest in age and his best friend.

Now Brett stood at the graveside with the preacher, listening to the kind words spoken about a man he hadn't known very well. It appeared Brett and the bartender from the saloon were the only ones who came to pay respects. It didn't matter because Brett had kept his word and that's what was important.

The deed crinkled in his pocket. As though shaking itself like some kind of burlesque dancer waving her female charms at him, trying to push Brett into going to the ranch, but he resisted. Something else Brett was good at.

After the service, the grave was filled in, and Brett said his thanks to the preacher. Brett and Mike went down to the saloon to have a whiskey and salute Martin, who had been a good customer. Hours passed while they talked and had a few more whiskeys. Finally, mid-afternoon rolled around and Brett broke free from Mike without being too conspicuous. Truth was, Brett'd already been to the lawyer in town and verified the ranch was his in legal terms. Martin had signed it over to him. Brett had nothing to worry about, nothing to hide, yet he still kept the information to himself.

Growing up with five brothers and one sister made it hard to have anything for himself. Maybe that's why he didn't tell anyone. There were no secrets, no special items that didn't get shared, taken or broken. It was just the way of things when you had so many siblings.

After leaving the saloon, Brett headed out toward the ranch, a bubble of excitement building inside him. He wasn't the type of man to get overly eager, to be goofy like his younger brother Jack, angry like his older brother Ray, or charming like Trevor. Brett simply stood in the shadows, watching, waiting, knowing one day his chance would come.

Today was that day. An unexpected grin curled his lips. He leaned low on the horse and urged it into a gallop, flying across the miles to get to the ranch as fast as he could. When it came into view, he thought perhaps he was seeing things.

When he finally rode into the yard, he realized it wasn't as bad as he thought. It was much, much worse.

Brett looked around at the sagging roof, the barn leaning to one side, missing boards, rotted boards poking out, evidence of many critters inhabiting the buildings. It had been quite some time since Martin had anything besides his old nag in that corral. Half the posts were broken or missing. Some of the cross-beams were in the same condition. The joy and excitement disappeared in a blink.

Brett's dream ranch was more like a nightmare.

Chapter One

July 1889

"I need to get married."

As soon as the words left Brett's mouth, he felt the truth of them like a mule kick.

Kincaid's dark brows rose. "I hope you're not considering me."

Brett rolled his eyes. "Not hardly. I mean now that I'm finally starting my own ranch, I need a wife. A good one, who won't drive me to the whores in town."

"I suppose that's what lots of men want."

They cleaned out the fireplace—what looked to be burned-up pieces of a table and chairs—and carried the charred wood outside. As they piled on the trash from inside the house, Brett thought more and more about what exactly he did want. A home, a wife, children probably. His brothers and sister certainly enjoyed all of that. He wanted what they had. He wanted it all. The fiasco with Adelaide and his brother Trevor in Cheyenne had taught Brett a valuable lesson.

It was all about love, and choosing the right woman.

As they walked into the bedrooms, they discovered a rope mattress made of straw holding a city-full of mice and enough of their droppings to fertilize an acre of corn. Brett and Kincaid dragged it all outside and threw it into a big pile. Mice scattered everywhere.

Brett shook his head. "The woman I want is not just another girl. She's a doctor."

"A doctor?" Kincaid coughed as the mattress hit the dirt.

"Yep, the town doctor. Used to be her pa's job, but he took sick a while back. Now she's it."

He'd spent a good portion of his youth following after Alex. Everyone always assumed they'd marry after Brett finally caught her. The truth was, Brett had been working up the nerve to ask her to marry him when things changed. When the foreman unexpectedly died, ranch duties kept him away from town for weeks on end. During that time, Alex made her choice to walk away from what they had and Brett had lived with it since.

He was going to change that starting now.

Brett stepped back into the house and pictured Alex Brighton in the kitchen. The curvy blonde had everything he wanted in a wife. Even though the place was dusty and dirty, and smelled like mouse shit, it felt good to stand in his own house. Soon it would be a home.

After Brett and Kincaid finished going through the house, they were both covered with dirt. Kincaid looked down at himself and frowned.

"I was planning on visiting a lady in town, but I'm gonna need to go take a bath before I do that."

Brett caught a whiff of his own stench and realized he had the same problem. He couldn't go courting Alex like this, but he and Kincaid had to finish what they started. Then they could go to town and get cleaned up. He wondered if Alex would be surprised to see him.

"All right, let's go check out that barn. Hopefully it won't fall over on us."

Kincaid chuckled. "I didn't know you were funny, Brett."

"I wasn't being funny."

The barn was in much worse shape than the house, if that was even possible. The doors hung cockeyed on the hinges. Of course, it was full of musty, moldy hay and God knows how many kinds of scat from God knows how many different kinds of animals. Some of them large, judging by the size of the tracks. Brett even spotted a few coyote and cougar tracks. The big creatures were long gone since there wasn't anything to eat in the barn.

Each of the stalls carried its own evil gift. Some of them held broken pieces of tack, others held mildewed straw, in another a couple of carcasses of a raccoon and squirrel. Apparently there'd been a small fire at one point given that there was a gaping, charred hole in the back of the barn. The loft was a total loss. The boards were rotted and pitted, and more than likely had never been replaced.

The whole thing looked to be as old as Martin, and perhaps it was. They certainly wouldn't be keeping their horses in that barn anytime soon. Thankfully it was the middle of summer, and it would be a long while before winter's fury was felt. Hopefully he had enough time and money to fix up the barn so it would be usable.

By the time they finished, Brett was more than ready to get to town. Once he'd thought things through and come to a decision, he wanted to take action. It was time to go see Alex. However, he had one stop to make first. A stop he dreaded.

His parents. Brett loved them dearly, but he had to let them know about the Square One. He hoped they understood his need to have his own ranch and break free from the family's yoke, or it would be hard going without their approval.

"I need to go over to my parents' before I go into town. You're welcome to come with me or you could head straight to town and I'll meet you there."

Kincaid nodded. "I think I'll just head straight to town. I don't do well with parents," he said with a wry grin.

"What say I meet you in town at the saloon, look for a bartender by the name of Mike. In about three hours?"

"Sounds good. Anything I should look out for?" Kincaid mounted his horse.

Brett knew what he was asking. Anyone in town who would take Kincaid's presence as an unfriendly act.

"Just tell them you're working for the Malloys. That should get you at least enough respect to get a whiskey or two."

"Okay, that's what I'll do then. I'll see you in three hours." Kincaid galloped off toward town.

Brett spent the time on the way over to his parents' ranch thinking about what he'd say. He spent a lot of time contemplating everything. He hadn't decided if that was a good thing or not—but it didn't matter. That was just how he was. It was important that he chose the right words. When he rode into the Malloy ranch, instead of feeling like coming home, for the first time in his life, he felt like a visitor. Like he'd come to call—a very strange feeling.

Almost foreign. Maybe because he'd spent the night camping out at the Square One or maybe because he'd been gone from home for so long. He'd spent an entire month in Cheyenne helping Trevor and Adelaide. He didn't know for certain exactly what had changed, but suddenly his home was no longer the Malloy ranch, it was someplace else. That someplace was his future.

He rode up to the house, and his mother came out the door. Her green eyes lit with joy. Thank God somebody felt joy when they saw him. A petite woman with chestnut-colored hair, she looked small, but she was the backbone of the Malloy family.

"Mama."

"Oh, *cherie*, it is so good to see you. I did not know you would be home. I would have made something special for dinner."

"It's okay, Mama. I kind of came home unexpectedly."

"Where is Trevor?"

"It's a long story. He'll be staying in Cheyenne. I'm sure you'll hear the details from him."

She frowned. "I don't like the sound of that. Did you and your brother have an argument?"

"Something like that. Don't dig, Mama, please don't dig. Now's not the time."

Brett wasn't ready to talk to anyone about Trevor yet. He was still working through the hurt caused by their falling out.

"Okay, but you boys, you are men now. You can't argue like young boys anymore."

The boys and men conversation again. Geez. As he dismounted, his mother came to him. When his arms closed around her, she fit so neatly under his chin that his throat grew tight. The warmth from a simple mother's hug filled him, giving him the kind of boost he needed to be able to say what he'd come to say.

"Is Pa around?"

"He's in the barn. His favorite mare threw a shoe."

"Let's go see him. I have something I need to tell both of you."

14

Again his mother looked at him with suspicion in her eyes. "Now that doesn't sound good either. Did you bring home any good news? And is that a bruise under your eye?"

He'd almost forgotten about the parting gift from Trevor. "You don't miss anything do you?"

"Of course not and neither do you."

It was true. His mother was incredibly observant, a skill she'd instilled in all her children, the ability to read people and situations, to know how to handle anything. If only he knew how to handle telling them he was leaving the ranch for good. When they stepped into the darkness of the barn, he heard the shoeing hammer ringing and the low murmur of his father's voice as he soothed the horse.

"Pa?"

"Brett, that you?"

"Yes, sir."

"You're back from Cheyenne. About time. Summer is always crazy. Glad to have you home, boy."

As Brett walked back toward his father, his stomach cramped and his throat felt dry.

No, sir, it was definitely not going to be easy.

His father hadn't changed much since Brett had been a child. John Malloy was a big man, about the same size as all his sons. With dark brown hair and blue eyes, he had the hands of a man used to hard work. His grip was as steady and strong as his word. His father was a man who stood tall and proud. A tough role model to live up to.

"I've got something to tell both of you. Something I should have told you a long time ago but didn't." He shuffled his feet and forced himself to continue. "About two years ago, I won old Martin's ranch in a poker game."

"Brett, how could you take another man's property like that?" His mother frowned.

His father wasn't as surprised. "Hm, I heard that. I wondered if you were planning on telling us."

Brett had forgotten that his father was friends with old Martin. They were just so different the way they lived their lives, it was hard to remember they were only about ten years apart in age.

"John, you need to tell me these things. Brett, I don't think you should—"

"Please listen, Mama, okay?"

She held up both hands as if to tell him to proceed.

"With me being gone, I've realized that this ranch doesn't need me."

Both of his parents started to protest.

"Now hold on and listen. The hands have obviously done what they needed to do to keep this ranch running. With both Trevor and me gone, well, not Trevor since he didn't do too much—"

"Brett, it's not nice to pick on your brother when he's not here to defend himself."

"Fine, I won't mention Trevor again." Brett took a deep breath. "I'm not a kid anymore. I'm a man and I have a ranch to build. A place that can be my home. A place for me. The first time in my life that I've ever owned anything. That was truly mine."

"That's not true. We gave you many things. Love, food, a horse of your own. Brett, everything you had was always yours." His mother looked truly hurt by his implication.

Brett needed to make her understand. "Yes, but that all came from you and Pa. This, this is *mine*. I know it's kind of odd to have won it in a poker game, especially with a pair of deuces."

His father laughed. "Talk about a lucky deal."

Brett threaded his fingers with his mother's. "But, it's the first thing that's come to me that hasn't passed through Malloy hands. I want to make it mine. I want to rebuild it and make it into a workable ranch. Something that I can be proud of. Something that you can be proud of. Do you understand? Am I making any sense?"

"Yes, you're making perfect sense to me. I understand." His father nodded. "That's how I started this place. I had nothing but your mother, and then we had Raymond. You fixing to get yourself some hands for this ranch?"

"Don't worry. I've got somebody to work the ranch with me."

"I'll miss you, *cherie.*" His mother cupped his cheek. "What about a wife? You are old enough to be married and have babies of your own."

His heart kicked at the reminder of the one person he needed to go see. "I have someone in mind."

"Oh, really? Do I know her?"

Brett didn't want his mother interfering with his plans for Alex. The last thing he wanted was her running to town for some made-up reason just to play matchmaker. Brett wanted to win his bride on his own, not because his mother pushed Alex into it.

"Mama, let me do one thing at a time here. I'll let you know as soon as she says yes."

He was afraid it would take a while. God knows it had been years since he even talked to Alex Brighton, but she was the perfect choice to be his bride. Now he hoped she still didn't hate him. His plan wouldn't be complete without her.

Chapter Two

Brett's stomach jumped around like a pack of frogs. He went into the bathing parlor with a weak grin and enough money to get a good bath and a shave. Old Joe Miller who ran the place looked at him askance, but fortunately didn't ask any questions.

The water nearly scalded him, but Brett didn't complain. It was a hot bath, something he hadn't had in at least three days and with all the work he'd been doing, a necessary evil. He scrubbed himself almost raw, but all the dirt, muck and grime finally came off.

His hand shook as he toweled off and dressed. Approaching Alex had been the foremost thing on his mind other than the ranch, and he was this close to her. Just fifteen minutes and he'd be at her door.

He was nervous. Brett, a man who prided himself on self-control, was stupidly nervous. When Joe shaved him, Brett had to close his eyes to avoid the older man's prying gaze.

"Been gone a spell, Brett."

"Yes, but I'm back now." He didn't want to get into details with Joe about where he'd been or what he'd been doing.

Joe scraped the whiskers from Brett's face, the rasp of the razor echoing off the wood-planked walls. "Mind my asking why you're not getting cleaned up at home? Not that I mind the money."

"Just shave me, Joe, okay?" Brett was jumpy enough without actually talking about why he was there.

"A man's business is his own." Joe wiped the razor on the towel lying on his shoulder. "Just being neighborly."

Brett grunted and kept his eyes closed. Ten more minutes and he'd see Alex.

Damn frogs.

∽∾∽∾

Alex Brighton was sorting the supplies that had been delivered that morning when she heard the clinic door open. They didn't have a terribly busy physician's practice, but they did get their fair share of patients.

After retiring a year earlier, her father didn't spend much time in the clinic. Since their nurse only worked three mornings a week, Alex was alone and had to see to whomever came by. She set the counted bandages to one side and scribbled the amount on a scrap of paper before she went to see who had arrived. When she came around the corner, she was glad the doorjamb was in reach.

Brett Malloy.

Those eyes. Those blue, blue eyes hadn't changed at all since he was a little boy. He had to be the most beautiful man God had put on the Earth. Unfortunately, God had also made him the most taciturn, stubborn and quiet man ever created. Not to mention the biggest idiot.

Something about Brett had always rested on her heart. Alex couldn't even begin to explain it other than to say she felt connected to him at the deepest level. Some kind of invisible bond and every time she saw him, her mouth always went cotton dry.

His appearance resonated through her like a stone in a bucket, ripples fanning everywhere. For a moment, Alex couldn't respond. He'd broken her heart once, and she had never forgiven him for what he'd thrown away. Their future, their children, their chance. She could be polite, but that didn't mean she had to be friendly.

"Surprised to see you here, Brett."

He took off his hat and fiddled with it. It was one thing the Malloy boys all had—beautiful hands. Alex had spent a good deal of time remembering those hands, how they felt on her skin, how the calluses made her nipples pebble.

Dammit, woman, get your thoughts in order.

"Good afternoon, Alex."

The clean scent of soap and his damp hair told her Brett had just bathed. More than likely down at Joe's place. That was unusual—why hadn't he bathed at home?

"What can I do for you?"

"Oh, yeah, I need supplies. Bandages, some betadine. Um, you know, whatever, um..."

Alex was at a total loss. The few words that came out of Brett Malloy's mouth were usually very thought out and as precise as the edge of a knife. This stumbling, bumbling Brett was completely unexpected. She didn't know what to make of it.

"Is anything wrong at home? Does your mother need supplies?"

"No, no, I'm starting my own place. Old Martin's ranch is mine now. And I just, uh, want to be ready, you know, for emergencies and so on."

"Oh, old Martin's place. I hadn't realized it had been sold."

That certainly made him uncomfortable. Alex swore his cheeks turned just the slightest shade of pink. Embarrassed? That was interesting. He didn't ever show much emotion, something that had always angered her, but this little tidbit made her want to snicker. With glee.

"Yeah, I um, I mean, I didn't buy it. Truth is that I got it from Martin about two years ago before he passed and uh, I'm just now getting around to getting it going."

"I'll just go put together a box full of medical supplies for the ranch. Won't be a couple of minutes." *Then you get your fanny out of here.* The longer Brett was here, the more likely she'd haul off and smack him.

"My thanks."

"Sit in the waiting area. You're just looking for some betadine, bandages and such for everyday needs?"

"Yes, and if you have a needle and some of that thread you use for stitches that'd be most helpful too." He sat in one of the straight back chairs in the waiting room.

As Alex went back into the supply room, she was dismayed to realize her hands were shaking. Dammit. Although she could've chosen any one of the Malloy brothers to become obsessed with, she got stuck with Brett.

Quiet Brett. Uncommunicative Brett.

After she gathered the supplies, she pushed them haphazardly into one of the boxes from the recent shipment, just to tuck everything together. Had she wanted more than a visit from a citizen to the town doctor? No, absolutely not.

Then why was she angry with him? It wasn't as if he'd ended their relationship yesterday. It was a lifetime ago. She'd gotten over him, hadn't she? Alex learned a valuable lesson with

Brett and had yet to give her heart over to another man. Being a physician was more than enough to make her life complete.

Maybe she believed it too. Or maybe she'd wanted Brett to come back on his hands and knees and apologize. Now that was laughable. Brett wouldn't get on his knees for anyone or anything.

After arguing with herself for several minutes, Alex decided to stop dilly-dallying and get rid of Brett. Just seeing him shouldn't send her into such a tizzy.

As she stepped back into the waiting area, her stomach did a flip-flop when she saw Brett wasn't alone. A dark-eyed man stood with him. A gunman if she were to guess. Anyone who wore two guns slung low on their hips was definitely a gunman in her opinion. He was tall like Brett, but thinner and lankier.

"Doctor Brighton, this is Kincaid. He'll be helping me out at the ranch for a while. Kincaid, this is the town doctor."

Kincaid smiled. "So this is your girl. If I had known y'all had a doctor who looked like her, I would've been here sooner."

Alex frowned at Brett who appeared as surprised as she was. "I'm not Brett's anything. Is Kincaid a first name or a last name?"

Kincaid shook his head. "It's my only name."

Her gaze locked with Brett's and Alex saw something that looked like jealousy, a shimmering spark of the vicious emotion which had ruined more than one life. Unexpected for sure since he was usually so cold and logical. He certainly had nothing to be jealous about though. She wasn't his anymore so he could just keep his opinion on that to himself.

"Should we be going?" Kincaid glanced at Brett and inclined his head to the door. "Got a few more places to visit."

"Oh, right." Brett reached for the box of supplies. "How much do I owe you, Alex?"

"Dollar and eighty-five cents." *Then get going.*

He pulled out some wadded bills from his pocket. Alex's gaze dropped to his trousers, a well-worn pair of denims that hugged him, reminding her he didn't have one ounce of fat on his body. He was hard all over.

A shiver wormed its way through her. It took serious self-control not to let them see it. She thought she'd gotten over Brett, at least her head had, now if only her body would follow suit. As he handed her the money, their fingers briefly touched and a tingle raced up her arm and down her shoulder to spread through her body. Both men tipped their hats and said good day.

After Kincaid stepped outside, Alex was alone with Brett, who looked at her with a fierce frown on his face.

"What?"

"Um, nothing. I just, it's been a while since I've seen you, Alex. You just...it's good to see you. I've missed you."

A searing flame of anger licked her. The past hurts combined with the present annoyance and almost burned her. Brett had *no* right to come in here and confuse her. Regardless if she sounded like a crazy shrew, Alex wouldn't stand for it.

"I don't even want to hear that from you. You lost that right twelve years ago."

His face appeared no less intense. "I'm sorry."

"Too little and too late. The door is behind you."

Alex took particular pleasure in noting that Brett nearly tripped on his way out the door. After the grin faded from her face, she clenched her fists in frustration. She wasn't a young girl or an empty-headed, silly, giggling fool—she was a woman.

A woman who refused to give into any longings her body might have for the man who'd shattered her heart.

She slammed the door and stood there with her pulse pounding, warning her stupid heart to slow down. Brett wasn't worth a moment of worry. He'd come by for bandages, that's all. Anything else wasn't worth contemplating.

Brett could have kicked his own ass. He'd behaved like a complete moron inside, stumbling over his words, and lying about why he was there. Something possessed his tongue and refused to allow it to work properly. She'd looked at him as if he'd lost his mind. Perhaps he had. He'd certainly acted like it.

Fool. Idiot.

"I thought you said you wanted to marry her?" Kincaid sounded amused as they untied their horses from the hitching post in front of Alex's house.

"Shut up."

The teeth of jealousy had bitten deep when Kincaid flirted with her. The green-eyed monster was unexpected and made him see red. Brett wasn't known for his temper, except when he lost it. Something that didn't happen often. Somehow just the smile Alex had bestowed on Kincaid nearly turned him into a snarling idiot.

Over the last five years, he hadn't said more than a dozen words to her, had actually avoided her. But now, everything was different; he was different and he wanted to be with her again. Getting her to marry him wouldn't be easy, and starting out with such an inauspicious beginning wouldn't help matters either. He couldn't afford to act like an idiot anymore if he wanted Alex for his wife.

Kincaid chuckled. "Sounds like you've got some work to do, cowboy."

That was an understatement of enormous proportions. Judging from the cold way she'd treated him, he'd need a goddamn bonfire the size of Texas to melt her. Alex was the perfect choice for a wife. Smart, beautiful in a non-traditional way with her open face and chocolate brown eyes, she had always been way more than he could ever hope to have. Hell, she was smarter than he and his brothers put together. Alex had everything—looks, brains, a bright future. Much more than a simple cowboy who made forty dollars a month could offer. Now he just had to get his foot out of his mouth and start acting like a man instead of a fool.

"I thought you were supposed to meet me at the saloon," Brett grumped at Kincaid as they rode down the street.

Kincaid shrugged. "I was on my way when I saw your horse. Figured I'd stop and see if you were ready."

Brett blew out a breath, wishing he could go back and relive the last twenty minutes. "Let's go down and see Mike, I need a drink."

೫೫೦೮

After a stop in the saloon, Brett and Kincaid spent the afternoon getting supplies and piling everything into the borrowed wagon. As they loaded up the last of the nails for the roof in small barrels, along with the tar, Kincaid broke the silence.

"So, this doctor lady, she really your girl?"

Brett's back went up and any good feelings he'd had for Kincaid flew away. "Why?"

"She's pretty, very nice, obviously a smart lady. Think somebody like me doesn't have a chance with her?"

"I didn't say that. I just asked a question."

"Well, so did I."

It was like two bucks butting horns over a doe. No way in hell he'd let Kincaid ruin his plans with Alex, even if she didn't know about them yet.

"She's mine," he snapped. "I told you I'm going to marry her."

Brett didn't know who was more surprised, Kincaid or him.

"Just asking. I'm guessing there's more single gals in town who aren't old women or whores."

"There's definitely other women in town. I'll be happy to introduce you." As long as he stayed away from Alex, Brett didn't give a shit who Kincaid courted.

After one last, fierce look, Kincaid shrugged and the moment was gone. Brett didn't want to fight with him, but for Alex, he'd do what he needed to.

It was close to late afternoon by the time they pulled up to the Square One ranch. His brother Raymond waited with a scowl on his face. He favored their mother in coloring with his green eyes, his hair a shade lighter than Brett's although they were similar in build. At the moment, Raymond's scowl wasn't as deep as it could go, but he sure as hell wasn't smiling.

"Hello, Ray."

"Brett. Who's your friend?"

"This is Kincaid."

Ray nodded and stepped off the front porch to greet them. Kincaid dismounted and stuck his hand out. Ray shook it politely as his eyes assessed the ex-gunslinger with sharp clarity. His intense gaze missed nothing.

"Tyler tells me you used to be a gunslinger. That's behind you now, right?"

Kincaid's eyebrows went up. "And if it isn't?"

"Well then no matter what my little brother says, you're not working on a Malloy ranch."

Kincaid turned to look at Brett, his stance, his arms, his hands, everything, at the ready. "That true, Brett?"

Brett stepped between them, looking his brother square in the eye. "You might be my big brother, Ray, but you sure as hell aren't my boss. Kincaid is here at my invitation. He is working my ranch, not yours. It doesn't matter one way or the other if he's working as a gunslinger or not. If you don't like it, you can get your ass off the property and come back when you can accept it."

Ray's expression didn't change. "Lily tells me that I need to be a little more kind to folks."

His wife was a smart woman, however Brett thought Ray's declaration was an understatement.

"I respect the fact that you want to run your own ranch." Ray pointed at Brett. "I just want to make sure everyone, including you, is safe."

"We're safe," Brett assured him. "Except maybe from the mouse shit that seems to have gotten ground into the floorboards in the house."

It seemed to break the tension, in fact, Ray almost smiled. He didn't smile often so it meant a lot that his mouth even twitched.

"Okay, I'm going to respect your opinion on this, baby brother, but I'm going to be watching. So your ranch ought to get used to me."

"I don't think anybody has ever gotten used to you, Ray, except Lily and she's a saint."

That earned another mouth twitch. "I'm not going to argue with you. I'm just lucky I found her when I did."

Another happily married Malloy. Brett was the only holdout. Ray glanced at the overfull wagon and whistled.

"You spent some of your funds."

"I surely did."

"I've got a pair of hands. I can help you unload."

"Thanks, I could use the help. Especially since I don't have to pay you."

Ray grunted and slapped him on the back. "Let's get busy."

The three of them worked for the next several hours to unload the wagon and put all the supplies in the appropriate places. During that time, Kincaid and Ray didn't speak much. There wasn't much conversation at all other than, "Where should I put this?" and, "Does that go there?"

It was close to sundown when they finally finished putting everything away. Brett looked at the house and was pleased to see he had the makings of his own home. Now he just needed to clean it so they could sleep under a roof that night. Fortunately he'd had a broom on his list and had picked one up at the general store along with buckets, scrub brushes and some lye soap.

Earlier that morning, when he checked the well, he was glad to see that the water was clear and fresh. After they cleaned up the old cookstove, they could heat some water and scrub the shit out of everything. Literally. He glanced at Ray.

"Don't suppose you're actually going to stick around and clean are you?"

"I'm gonna have to pass on that particular pleasure. Lily's expecting me for supper."

"I didn't think so." As they walked out together, Brett noted Kincaid had picked up a rag and oil and started cleaning the stove. He'd say one thing for the ex-gunslinger, the man put in a serious hard day's work.

When Brett and Ray got outside, Ray closed the door behind them. "You sure you can trust this man?"

"I think so. Certainly more than I trust most folks." Brett had a hard time with trust in general. No need to sugarcoat it for his brother. He owed him the truth.

"Fine then, but I will be checking on you. If you need help, you just let me know."

"Always the big brother, always the protector."

Ray couldn't help but look out for his younger siblings. In a way, it touched Brett. Even though the sentiment was half-assed, and said as a bit of a threat, it still touched him.

Brett shook his brother's hand and gave him a quick hug, shocking the hell out of both of them.

"Uh, I'll see you then."

"Thanks again, Ray. Tell Lily and Melody I said hello."

"I'll surely do that. Have a good night in your new house, and congratulations, little brother."

As Ray rode away, Brett decided he'd do just that. A good night in his new house. Tomorrow he'd begin his courting in earnest. Alex would be his before the first snowfall.

Chapter Three

The problem with King Dawson was that his parents had raised him to be one. A more arrogant, pompous windbag could not be found in Wyoming. Growing up, King was the type of boy who liked to burn ants with a magnifying glass and pull the wings off flies. Alex felt certain that King had been responsible for the death of her cat Jingles when she and King were ten.

King had been married and widowed twice already. Fortunately no children had resulted from the marriages. Alex had always wondered if the reason Millie and Bernice Dawson had died was due to King's need to produce children. An unkind thought, but they'd both suffered multiple miscarriages and they hadn't become pregnant on their own. King seemed to think his wealth and his supposed esteemed status in the social circles of Cheshire made him a good catch. No matter how many times Alex politely turned him down for his weekly invitations to come out and visit his estate, he still kept coming back.

She was not surprised to see him only a few days after his last unsuccessful attempt at wooing her. Alex was stitching a cut on Slim Murphy's hand. The old cowpoke had grabbed hold of barbed wire without his gloves and torn up his palm pretty badly. He only winced once or twice during the procedure. To keep his mind off it, she flirted with him a bit knowing the older man would not take her seriously. He knew she had his best interest at heart and his pride foremost in her mind.

The door slammed open and Alex did all she could not to jump. Something told her it was King.

"Alexandra." His booming voice echoed through the clinic, loud enough to wake her father who snored peacefully in his bedroom upstairs.

She ignored King and put the last stitch on Slim's hand. "That wasn't too bad, was it?"

The silver-haired man gave her a weak grin. "Yep, it was, but I reckon I ain't gonna complain about it. Better than losing my hand."

"That it is." As she began to clean the residual blood off his hand, the door to the examining room burst open.

"Mr. Dawson," she said with a snap in her voice. "This is a private examining room. You may not simply come in when you feel like it. Please go back out into the waiting room and *wait.*"

"Alexandra, is that any way to talk to your future husband?"

She rolled her eyes at Slim and he bit back a grin. "Mr. Dawson, wait in the waiting room."

"Well I'll do it since you asked so politely." King finally retreated from the room.

With a sigh, Alex shook her head and started to wrap the bandage around Slim's hand.

"That fella surely does want to marry you, Doc. Why wouldn't you want to marry a man with that much money?"

"Slim, have you met King Dawson?"

"A time or two."

"There you have it. If you know King then you know the answer to that question."

This time Slim did laugh and she was pleased to note he had a little more color in his cheeks.

She handed him extra bandages. "Now keep that clean and change the bandage at least once a day. I'm sure Mrs. Fielding will help you."

Mrs. Fielding was the cook at the ranch where Slim worked. She had some nursing skills, almost needed to with all the men out there. Casey's ranch was the second largest in the area with at least sixty men at any given time. Mrs. Fielding was a busy woman.

"Thank you kindly, Doc. How much do I owe you?"

"We'll just call it eight bits and we'll be even."

He eyed her suspiciously. "That doesn't sound like too much for all you just did."

"That's okay. Every time a handsome man comes to call, I don't charge him very much."

He patted her shoulder. "You're a good woman, Doc Brighton."

"Thank you, Slim."

She escorted him out the door and went to go face King in the waiting room. A task she was definitely not looking forward to.

When Alex stepped into the parlor, the sheer size of King overwhelmed the space. His two ever-present armed men stood by the door. King must have some kind of Viking ancestry because he easily stood six and half feet tall, shoulders twice as wide as a normal man's. His thick, shaggy blond hair topped a square, rough-hewn face and blue eyes. Not the kind of blue that Brett had, more of an icy blue.

Dang it, she had to stop thinking about Brett.

King wore his favorite outfit—a blue chambray shirt with a string tie, and a suit jacket with fancy trousers, along with his boots. She thought they looked like alligator skin but she wasn't quite certain. He told all and sundry that they had cost him a small fortune to order them from New York.

King acted like the royalty of Cheshire—he'd inherited the largest ranch. Although he had money, that didn't make him royalty in Alex's eyes. Half the town kowtowed to him. The other half tried to stay out of his path.

He filled the silver brocade settee in the corner of the parlor. Although she'd told him to sit in the waiting room, he chose to invade the family's parlor instead. Typical King behavior. His arms reached from one side to the other as he sat like a king on his throne. She put her hands on her hips and looked at him with her sternest expression.

"If I have a patient, the door is closed for a reason. You are not to invade someone's privacy."

He scoffed. "Pshaw. It was just that old fool Slim. What did he do, cut up his hand on barbed wire again? Casey ought to fire him."

"What his injury was is none of your concern. I am his doctor, therefore it's my business to protect him. You'd better not go talking to Casey about firing him because he came to see me."

"Only because you asked me to, darlin'."

"Don't make me repeat myself, King. Do *not* call me darlin'. I am not, nor will I ever be, your darling."

He stood, towering over her. Alex refused to be intimidated by his size. He cupped her face in his dinner-plate-sized hands.

"Aw, Alex, you know we're gonna get hitched one day."

She stepped away from him, pleased to note that her body had no reaction to his touch. Not the reaction he was hoping for anyway. Alex suppressed the urge to wash and rid herself of the lingering disgust from the touch of his hands.

"What makes you think that I'm going to change my mind after ten years of saying no?"

"Because you will."

King justified anything he wanted to by simply saying it was so. Not an unusual occurrence.

"Why are you here?" She tried not to be rude but sometimes King pushed her patience too far.

"I hear Brett Malloy owns old Martin's place."

News traveled fast in a small town. She didn't bother to ask where he'd gotten the information.

"I also hear that he's got some kind of gunslinger working for him. Is he expecting trouble?"

"Why are you asking me?" Alex frowned.

"Because I hear the first place he went when he came into town was to see you. It's no secret he's always wanted you for his own. It's also no secret he knows you're mine."

"Oh for pity's sake, King. I am nobody's. I am my own person, not a piece of property to be bartered or traded or held up like a trophy. Now, I will tell you so you don't go shooting off at the mouth with rumors and gossip. Yes, Brett is now the owner of old Martin's place, in fact he's owned it for two years. The gunslinger is a friend of his working as a ranch hand, not as a gunslinger. I expect they've got a lot of work to do so you best leave them alone. They're no threat to you or your hundred thousand acres." She took a breath. "Now if you're not here for a medical reason, please leave."

"How did he get it?"

Beth Williamson

"What are you talking about?"

"How did he get the ranch two years ago? Old Martin didn't keel over until a year ago. Did he own it when Martin still lived there?"

Alex really hadn't thought about that, but it was true. If Brett had owned it two years ago, Martin had still been alive at the time. She'd be curious to know exactly how Brett became the owner of the property, however she wasn't about to let King suck her into his gossip circle.

"The answers to your questions are not here. I'm fairly certain you've already checked to be sure he's the legal owner."

A quick flash of guilt in those cool eyes told her that was truth.

"Then just let him be." She walked to the door and opened it, gesturing for him to leave. "If you don't mind."

King hitched up his pants and swaggered toward her. She had to bite back a smile. Sometimes his antics, although not meant to be, were entirely comical.

"I'm just going to let Malloy know that you're mine, Alex."

She opened her mouth to refute him yet again, and he put two fingers across her lips.

"You're *mine*."

A low growl echoed through the foyer. King leveled a narrowed gaze at Alex's dog Ug. The medium-sized mutt looked ready to attack with his teeth bared and his mud-colored fur standing on end.

"I hate that dog."

"I think the feeling is mutual."

Ug barked until King's hands left Alex's skin. Then the dog stepped up to her side and pressed against her leg.

"That's the ugliest dog I've ever seen."

36

"Ug doesn't have to be pretty. He's a good dog."

She'd found him in the alley next to the clinic, near death, about five years ago. Not an animal doctor, she did her best to save him from his serious wounds. Someone had obviously used the dog for kicking practice. After he'd miraculously healed, Ug became her dog, protecting her, comforting her, her steady friend in a lonely world.

She'd named him Ug after everyone in town called him Ugly. He definitely had good taste because he hated King.

"You're still mine, Alex. No one can change that fact. Not even that butt-ugly mutt of yours."

Chapter Four

"Now that's one great big son of a bitch."

Brett looked up through the sweat-soaked hair hanging before his eyes to see King Dawson riding toward them. The man never rode alone. Two men rode about a hundred yards behind him—his second level of defense. Not that he needed any with his size.

"Shit."

He'd never liked King, who acted as if the world should fall at his feet simply because of his royal name. He was an arrogant ass. Not only that, he'd been sniffing after Alex for years, even though he'd been married twice. The way King went about life annoyed the hell out of Brett.

He sighed, set down the hammer and sat back on the roof, waiting for King to arrive.

"Friend of yours?"

Brett looked at Kincaid. "No, but he's rich."

"I know the type," Kincaid said as he kept on hammering.

They were nearly done fixing the roof on the house. A tree branch or something had damaged the north side. Before it rained, Brett wanted to get the holes fixed and repair any other damage to the roof. Then they could work on finishing the inside.

He wiped his brow with the sleeve of his shirt. Although still early in the day, it was hot. And would only get hotter.

King rode straight toward them on his palomino. The man was so big, his feet hung only eighteen inches off the ground. Not too many horses could carry a man of his size.

"Malloy," he called up.

"Dawson."

King looked around as if surveying a property for sale. "Looks like you're fixing it up."

"You've got keen eyes there, King."

King's gaze narrowed, apparently unsure if he'd been insulted or not. "I hear tell that you're the new owner of this ranch."

Brett wasn't sure where King was going with his line of questions. "You heard right. It's mine."

"You know, old Martin had two sons."

Fortunately for Brett he already knew that judging from the things left in the house. They'd found a child-size bed and another narrow, longer bed, a child's top, a checker, and what looked like the remnants of a small wooden horse. They surmised that two children had lived there, not one. However he'd have been shocked if just learning the information. He suspected some kind of dirty laundry lurked in Martin's life that had yet to be brought to light. Brett hadn't known Martin had a family. Certainly not in the last twenty-five years since Brett remembered first seeing him. "What's your point, King?"

"The ranch should have gone to his older son."

Brett picked up his hammer. "I've got a lot of work to do. If you came out here for a reason, spit it out. I can't stand here jawing with you all day. I'm sure you've already checked and figured out that I've owned this ranch for two years."

While he didn't want to anger anyone, he wasn't about to take a shovelful of shit from King Dawson.

"Stay away from Alexandra."

Brett almost dropped the hammer. "What does that mean?"

King leaned forward in the saddle, the creak of leather protesting the big man's weight. "Just what I said. She's mine and you don't need to be sniffing around her skirts no more."

"That's ridiculous. She's not yours," Brett scoffed. "She's not married to you or anyone. The only person who has a claim on Alex Brighton is Alex Brighton." If Brett had any say in it, soon she would be Alex Malloy and he'd have that claim on her.

"That's a load of manure. No woman should be in charge of herself. Soon as that old coot kicks the bucket, she'll be running to me." King smiled, pleased with himself.

Choosing not to respond, Brett continued to hammer.

"Now that we've got that cleared up, I just wanted to let y'all know my spread is right east of here."

"Yes, I did know that." Brett's patience got thinner.

"That means we're neighbors. If you happen to see any of my cattle wander over onto your thousand acres, I'm sure you'd spot them pretty much immediately. Just send them on back. You know what the brand looks like right?"

Everyone knew what the brand looked like. King had fashioned a brand from a capital D with spikes on it that resembled a crown.

"Sure do. Thanks for stopping by, King. Don't let us keep you."

King's gaze flickered to Kincaid. "This that gunslinger I heard about?"

That was it. Brett's patience snapped. "King, this is my friend, Kincaid. He's working my ranch with me for a while.

Kincaid this is King Dawson. He's the pompous bastard who owns the ranch east of here, who obviously likes to gossip and mind everyone else's business."

King's sly expression turned thunderous. "Who the fuck do you think you're talking to? I own this town."

"The only thing you own is the right to be an ass, which I'm not going to stop you from doing because you're so good at it. Now get off my land."

King stared at him hard. "You sure you want to do this, Malloy?"

It was a warning, of sorts. A warning from a big boot to an ant, as if to say, "I can squash you any time I want."

Was Brett sure? No, he wasn't, but somehow telling King Dawson to get off his land felt so good, almost to the point of a sexual release. He'd been a bully all of Brett's life and for once, Brett wasn't going to walk away. He had something now that was his and he wasn't about to let just anyone come onto his property unless they were there for friendly reasons. King's visit could never be termed friendly.

Brett's answer was to turn his back and start hammering. The next thing he heard was hoofbeats as King rode away.

"Well, he's a nice, welcoming neighbor."

Brett chuckled. "I told you he was a pompous ass."

"You seem to like to use that word for him. Now I'm only going to think of him as King Ass," Kincaid said with a slice of humor in his voice.

Shaking his head, Brett continued to hammer. In the back of his mind, he wondered how King knew that old Martin had a son, and exactly what he knew about the son. When Brett wasn't thinking about that, he was thinking about Alex.

Alex remained firmly entrenched in his mind, no matter how much he tried to focus on what he was supposed to be doing. It had been four days since he'd seen her, and he wondered if she thought about it as much as he did. Not likely, except if she was stewing about it. Brett had ruined the first chance he had, now he was in danger of ruining the second.

Brett knew he should be paying attention to what he was doing. Unfortunately when one doesn't pay attention to what they're doing, and what they're doing requires one to pay attention, accidents happen.

It was late afternoon and Brett walked around below the eaves, checking out the work they'd done on the roof. He heard Kincaid shout his name, seconds before something slammed into his shoulder. It more or less felt like a rock, then something equally heavy slammed into his head and all went black.

CR80BO

"Dammit, wake up, Malloy. I don't need your family thinking I killed you." Kincaid's annoyed voice broke through the fog surrounding Brett.

A trickle of cool water touched his mouth. He lapped at it as best he could while an entire church of screeching bells clanged in his head. Brett tried to sit up and agony ripped through him from head to toe. As he struggled for breath, he realized the sticky warmth on his neck was too thick to be sweat. He reached back and swiped at the sticky liquid. When he forced his eyes open, crimson met his gaze.

He heard Kincaid say, "Oh, shit. Well, I guess you're going to see your doc lady friend sooner than you thought."

Kincaid's face suddenly appeared in front of him, his brows drawn together. "I don't know what the hell you were thinking. I was throwing the spare lumber off the roof, like I told you. Another six inches to the right and that board would've cut your head in half instead of just denting it. I don't know how much damage it did since I've come to the conclusion that your head is as hard as the wood. Probably as hard as granite. You sure as hell bleed pretty good though."

Brett sucked in a much-needed breath. "Damn that hurts."

"I don't doubt that. That blood pumping out of your shoulder and head sure do tell a story. You're gonna need some stitches, boy."

Brett's gaze refused to do anything but see a blurry world. "You'd better bandage me up. Use one of those rags. Then we can ride into town and have the doc take a look at me."

Without a whole lot of finesse, Kincaid wrapped Brett's shoulder and tied it off, eliciting a groan Brett had been holding back through sheer force of will.

"That hurt?" Kincaid surveyed his handiwork.

"No, you idiot, it doesn't hurt."

Kincaid then wrapped Brett's head, a little bit more gently this time.

"Well at least you can still be sarcastic. You sit right there and I'll hitch up the horses. You do plan on taking the wagon, right?"

The pain warred with the dizziness. Brett hated the fact that his injury forced him to ride in the back of a wagon, but he knew he had no choice. "Wagon."

Brett waited with his eyes closed, glad, extremely glad, that he'd offered Kincaid a job. Not only was he a good worker, but he was turning out to be a good friend.

CS80CO

The last thing Alex expected to see when she opened the door was Kincaid supporting Brett. The entire left side of his body was covered in blood, his skin the color of milk, his gaze unfocused.

"Inside now. Straight to the examining room. Second door on the left." Her heart lodged in her throat at the sight of Brett so pale and bloody. She had to put her personal feelings, good or bad, aside and concentrate on helping the patient.

Kincaid helped Brett climb onto the examining table. There seemed to be copious amounts of blood. She wasn't sure if he had one wound or a hundred.

Kincaid frowned at Brett's chalky pallor. "What can I do?"

"Go the kitchen—it's at the end of the hall. On the stove you'll find a hot water reservoir. There's an enamel pot right on the stove keeping warm. Ladle some water into the pan and bring it back to me."

"Yes, ma'am." Kincaid left the room before she'd finished talking.

She looked at Brett, whose coloring was not good. "Do you feel woozy?"

"Alex," he said. "You have the most beautiful brown eyes."

Alex rolled her eyes. Apparently loss of blood turned Brett into a romantic lady's man.

She held up two fingers. "How many fingers am I holding up?"

"And your hands, your fingers are just so long, slender. Makes me want to lick them."

A jolt of energy flew through Alex, which had nothing to do with being a physician and everything to do with being a woman. Certainly an inopportune time for that to happen, particularly since she didn't want to feel that way over Brett.

Kincaid stepped back into the room with the water, his eyebrows up. "Did he just say he wanted to lick your fingers?"

Alex blushed. "Yes he did. Ah, but we're going to work on making sure he's okay. What happened?"

As Kincaid explained how Brett had been injured, Alex unwrapped the rag bandages, wincing at the sight of so much of Brett's blood.

"You did a good job with him, Mr. Kincaid. You not only bandaged it well, but it's a wonderful tourniquet on his arm. We need to get the bleeding stopped."

Alex took a deep breath and concentrated on helping a patient. She had to focus, it was the only way she could forget the fact that Brett lay bleeding on her table and avoid running from the room.

"I'm going to have to clean out the wounds and take out any debris that's left before I can stitch them. I'll be administering laudanum for the pain, although it seems to me he's out of his mind anyway. Probably from loss of blood."

Kincaid nodded. "What do you want me to do?"

"I'd like to give him a little water to wash the laudanum down. Would you get a glass from the kitchen please? Oh, and bring a spoon."

He was off again, confirming Alex's opinion that Kincaid wasn't a coldhearted gunslinger, otherwise he would have left Brett to die. Instead he chose to bring him in for treatment, and serve as her temporary nurse.

When Kincaid returned with the water, she carefully poured the exact dose of the drug into the glass and stirred it until it was mixed. She dribbled some of the concoction into Brett's mouth. His wandering gaze suddenly focused on her.

"That doesn't taste very good."

"Yes, but it will make you feel better. Just a little bit, Brett. Come on, open up."

He halfheartedly tried to push her away. "I know what that is and I don't want it."

"Sometimes in life we have to do what we don't want to do." She supported his head as he swallowed a small bit of water. "You'll feel better if you drink more of the water."

"For a doctor you sure are pushy."

Alex smiled. "Better me to be pushy than you be in pain."

Like a good patient, Brett swallowed the rest of the water, making a face the entire time. After he finished, she set the glass on the instrument table.

"Alex..."

"Yes, Brett?"

"I always wondered what it would be like to kiss you again."

Her cheeks burned a bit, and she hoped Kincaid hadn't noticed. "Shut up, Brett. Now just relax."

She caressed his brow until his eyes closed. Then she got to work.

As she began cleaning the wounds, she found bits of dirt, leaves and quite a few splinters. He must have been in agony. One splinter had to be two inches long. Kincaid stayed through it all. She was even pleased to note that he washed his hands when she did. Sterilizing the environment was incredibly important to her.

She tended the head wound first, making sure there wasn't any additional trauma. One gash bled profusely. With Kincaid's assistance, she shaved just enough of Brett's soft brown hair to stitch the wound closed. She rinsed the blood from the rest of his hair, making sure he had no other wounds. After applying a clean bandage, she set to work on the rest of him.

Although it wouldn't be a pretty scar on his shoulder, she made the stitches as small as she could. No doubt with Brett's healing power, he'd be back using his arm within a week or two. She wrapped the bandage around his shoulder, glad to note the wound was on his right arm. Since he was left-handed, he'd at least have use of his master hand.

As she cleaned up the bloody towels and water, Kincaid assisted without her even asking.

"You should be careful, Mr. Kincaid, someone might get the impression that you're kind or that you care about other people."

He looked a little startled. "I certainly don't want that to happen."

She smiled. "Thank you for helping Brett."

"Wasn't a problem, Doc. He's good folk."

"The Malloys certainly are." No need to go into her own opinion of Brett.

"And I didn't hear anything about wanting to kiss you," Kincaid teased.

"You'd better be careful or you'll be labeled a charmer." She laughed.

His face wiped clean of any emotion. "That's not going to happen anytime soon."

Unsure of what she'd said to offend him, Alex decided to change the subject as quickly as she could. "He'll probably be asleep for a few hours. I won't know the extent of any head trauma until he wakes up. I'm afraid he'll have to stay here for at least two days." Not exactly who she wanted to keep company with. "It's pretty close to suppertime, why don't you go down to the restaurant and get yourself something to eat."

"Only if I can bring something back for you."

"No, I'm all right. I've got food here. Don't worry about me."

"All right. I'll be back in the morning."

"Thank you again for your help, Mr. Kincaid. I truly, truly appreciate it."

She meant that. Without him, Brett surely would have bled to death before he reached her.

"You're welcome."

The dark-eyed man left her alone with Brett, who was sleeping peacefully on the examining table. He was still a bit pale. Alex had no idea how much blood he'd lost, but it was enough to sap his body of its natural golden complexion.

Alex got a blanket out of the linen closet and covered him from shoulder to foot. Once the laudanum wore off, he'd likely be cold. Seemingly of their own volition, her hands crept to his soft, wavy brown hair, careful to avoid his wound. It was like silk sliding through her fingers. She should be embarrassed about touching him when he wasn't awake, but it was as if something had a hold of her. She clenched her hand and backed away. Damn Brett Malloy for coming back into her life.

It wasn't a perfect life, but it was a good one. Now he had to muddy the waters again. She'd successfully avoided him for years and now she'd seen him twice in one week. Not only that, but she had to treat him, keep touching him. Torture. Goddamn torture.

If there was any mercy in the world, she'd only have to endure it for two days.

◌ଃ༄

Brett woke up slowly as if he swam in a sea of confusion, a sticky world of sounds, pain and fear. He tried to speak, but all that came out was a groan. His eyelids, heavier than lead weights, refused to work.

"Brett?"

He heard Alex's voice. Again he tried unsuccessfully to speak. "Uhhhhh."

"It's okay, you don't have to talk. I gave you something for the pain. It's wearing off. Take your time and don't force it. Do you know where you are? Nod your head if you do."

He nodded slightly and those bells clanged in his head. Mustn't do that again.

"You're in the examining room in the clinic. Mr. Kincaid brought you in with head and shoulder wounds, apparently from a piece of falling wood, which cut you up quite a bit. I've cleaned the wounds and sutured them. They look good and I think you will heal well."

Normally Brett would have protested against any woman taking care of him instead of the other way around. God knows he'd fought against his mother's fussing most of his life. When Alex said it, suddenly his apprehension, discomfort and downright fear dissipated.

"Wife."

He handed himself over to her care and slipped back into grayness.

Wife?

What in tarnation did that mean? Alex stared at the unconscious Brett for a bit before stepping back. Madness, that's what it was. The injury had knocked his brain loose.

Wife indeed.

Not in this lifetime. He'd made his choice and they both had to live with it. She wasn't about to relive that pain all over again. Nothing doing.

Cஜஐ80

Brett woke again, this time with a much clearer head, but an enormous headache that seemed to reverberate all the way to his toes. He opened his eyes and realized he was lying on the examining table in Alex's clinic. He caught a whiff of her unique scent and knew she was nearby.

"Alex?" It came out as more of a croak, but at least it was a noise.

She appeared beside him almost instantly, a sleep crease in her cheek. "How are you feeling?"

"Awful."

A furry head popped up beside her. That funny-looking dog that followed her around. What was his name again? Ug. That was it.

"I don't doubt it. You have a nasty wound on your head. Do you have any nausea or dizziness?"

Her cool hands felt his brow, then opened his eyes a bit wider. As she peered into them, he felt himself drowning in the depths of her gaze. Falling deeper, faster than he'd ever been. As his control slipped, he tried to grab onto it. He cleared his throat and the moment snapped. When she took her hands off him, he breathed a little easier.

"I'm a bit dizzy but my stomach feels fine." Though he had a feeling if he stood up he'd lose his breakfast.

"I was afraid of that. I think you have a concussion. You're going to need to stay here for a couple of days." She frowned, her eyebrows making an angry blonde V.

"No need to worry. I can go back home. Kincaid—"

She cut through the air with her hand, silencing him.

"I'm speaking as your doctor, Brett. Believe me, the last person I want in this clinic for two days is you." She walked over to the counter, tossing that remark over her shoulder.

"What does that mean?"

When she turned back, Alex's face had flushed a sweet shade of pink. "You know exactly what it means, Brett Malloy."

"Aw, Alex, you can't still be mad about—"

She waved her hand again and yelled, "Stop."

Brett winced and closed his eyes. Ug licked his left hand and uttered a small whine.

"Sorry about the shout. I'm not about to hear any gibberish from you about how I should feel. You had that chance and you threw it away." She hastily opened another blanket and threw it on top of him. "I'll be back to check on you in a few hours. Try to sleep."

With a bang of the door, Alex left him alone with the dog. Ug laid his paw on the cot and gazed at him with doggie understanding. Brett had been hoping she'd let bygones be bygones, but obviously not. Brett sighed. Now he'd really have to woo her.

Dammit.

ଓଛଠ୫

Bright sunlight filtered through Alex's window when she woke, groggy and irritable. Being stuck with Brett's company had turned her mood from chipper to foul. Then for him to tell her she couldn't still be mad...

Nothing doing. That was not going to happen. She had every right to be angry. Brett had made a choice that cost them their future together and she'd never forgive him for it. After she'd given everything to him, her heart, her soul, her body, he simply drifted away with no excuses or apologies. Just a letter that said, "I don't think we suit for marriage. I wish you luck. Brett." The very thought of that letter made her angry and sad at the same time. Her eyes tried to squeeze out a tear, but she refused to allow it to happen.

She'd cried oceans of tears over him. Never again.

After a quick wash and some clean clothes, Alex peeked into her father's room. He snored, tucked down into the covers. Hopefully he'd keep on sleeping and not add to her already high stress level. She headed downstairs as a knock sounded on the front door.

When she opened the door, Kincaid whipped off his hat.

"Morning, Doc."

"Good morning, Mr. Kincaid." She gestured for him to come in. "Brett woke up a couple of times last night. He's okay but he has a concussion and he's going to have to stay here for a couple of days."

Kincaid's eyebrows shot up. "You don't sound too happy about that. As near as I could tell you and him were...together."

Alex snorted so hard, she started coughing. Kincaid slapped her on the back and after a few moments, she was able to breathe again.

"I don't know what he's told you, but Brett and I haven't been together in twelve years. He ended it." Alex would have to question Brett on exactly what he was telling people and why.

"Really? So does that mean you'll have dinner with me?" Kincaid flashed a cocky grin.

"No, but thank you for asking."

He smiled. "No harm in asking. You're one fine-looking woman, Doc. A man would count himself lucky to have a gal like you."

Unbelievably, Alex felt her cheeks heat. "Thank you, Mr. Kincaid. Uh, would you like to see Brett?"

"Sure thing. I brought his horse by just in case. Left it at the livery with Will." Kincaid's boots thunked on the wood floor as he walked toward the examining room.

Alex looked in and saw Brett awake, staring at the ceiling. No doubt thinking of inventive ways to make her life more difficult.

"I'll leave you two to talk and go get the coffee on."

"Much obliged, Doc." Kincaid nodded and entered the examining room.

Alex proceeded to the kitchen, telling herself she wasn't running from Brett, but merely tending to her guest's needs.

"You're alive at least."

Brett glanced at Kincaid as he stepped toward him. He'd spent a hard night, alternating between a throbbing shoulder and an aching head. He scratched at the stitches beneath the bandage that decorated his right shoulder.

"You know you probably shouldn't be scratching at those."

He glared at Kincaid with a frown. "I don't need you to tell me what to do. I've got Alex for that."

"From what she tells me, she isn't your gal anymore." Kincaid grinned. "It's gonna be right interesting to watch you and Doc together. Especially since you told her she was so beautiful."

Brett's breath caught. "What the hell are you talking about?"

"Well...while you laid on that table bleeding like a stuck pig, you were telling the doc how you thought she was beautiful and that you always wanted to kiss her. And there was something about licking her fingers."

"I did no such thing," Brett protested loudly. His head repeated the protest.

Kincaid chuckled with evil glee. "Oh, yes you did. I was there. I heard all of it."

Brett threw a tongue depressor at Kincaid. It bounced off his chest, which just made Kincaid laugh harder.

"I did not tell Alex Brighton that she was beautiful."

"Okay, don't believe me. Ask her. Ask her what you said when you were out of your head. When folks are out of their head, that's when they're the most honest."

Brett's heart pounded. Did he really say those things to Alex? He didn't remember anything like that. In fact, the last thing he remembered clearly was climbing in the wagon and heading for town. After that he remembered waking up in the examining room, just a hazy memory of Alex's voice and her touch.

He also remembered the dog Ug and Alex changing his bandage before she left. He couldn't possibly have told her she was beautiful. Could he? Not something that Brett would normally say. Was Kincaid right? Had he already begun wooing her? More importantly, had it worked?

Chapter Five

Alex made scrambled eggs with a fierce frown. She could count the number of times she'd seen Brett in the last ten years on one hand, now he was with her for the next forty-eight hours. Lady Luck sure didn't like her. All Alex had to do was stay strong and forget the memories.

Forget the time they lay down in the tall grass by the creek on the Malloy property and made sweet love. Forget the first time he'd told her she was perfect for him. Forget the time he'd told her he could never marry her.

Oh, yep, that'd work.

"What did those eggs ever do to you?" Her father's voice broke through her angry meanderings.

"Papa. I'm sorry. I'm a little out of sorts this morning. We had a new patient come in and I was up a lot with him during the night." She wasn't lying to her father, just omitting the part about being sleepless because she was thinking about him recuperating downstairs.

"Really? What kind of injury?"

"Concussion, contusions and some lacerations. He seems to be fine, but with the head injury I thought he needed to stay here for a couple of days." Damn his sorry hide.

"Good idea." Her father's white hair stuck up every which way and his craggy face appeared to have sagged even lower. He wasn't well, nor was he taking care of himself. The liquor he consumed was beginning to consume him.

"Do you want some breakfast?"

He patted his stomach. "No, I'm not feeling up to it. I will take some coffee though."

She poured him a cup and wondered how she could convince the physician to heal himself.

"Thank you, sweetheart. I'll just go poke my head in and introduce myself." He started to walk out of the kitchen.

"Wait! It's, uh, well, that is..." She threw up her hands. "Okay, it's Brett."

He pursed his lips. "That is interesting. And you didn't kill him?"

"Funny, Papa. Very funny." She scraped the now overdone eggs onto the waiting plate. "He's a patient, nothing more."

"So I hear." He sounded anything but convinced.

"Here, bring him these." She thrust the plate at her father. "He can't have coffee but if he wants water or milk, let me know."

"Yes, ma'am." With another probing look, her father shuffled out of the kitchen.

Why couldn't Brett have bought a ranch in the next county? At least then she wouldn't worry about being his physician. She gripped the edge of the sink and willed herself to slow down and get control. Brett had always made her crazy, brought out the worst in her temper and temperament. Alex wasn't a violent person by nature, but there were times he drove her to it.

After a few deep breaths, she straightened. She wouldn't allow him to ruin what she'd worked hard to build. Brett wasn't going to change her life again.

"Dr. Byron." Brett was shocked to see how old and frail Alex's father looked. "It's good to see you. This is my friend Kincaid."

The old doctor nodded. "Good morning, gentlemen." He glanced down at the plate in his hands. "Alex made you some breakfast. At least I think it's breakfast. I'm not sure if she's trying to heal or harm here."

Kincaid chuckled. "Sounds like my kind of woman."

"Shut up." Brett tried to sit up but his head protested vehemently. "Holy cow."

"Lay back down and I'll feed you." Dr. Byron sat on the chair next to the examining table. "Makes me feel like I'm not entirely useless."

"You're as sharp as a tack." Brett didn't think Byron's mental faculties had changed one bit.

"More like dull as dishwater."

All three of them laughed. While Byron fed Brett the rubbery eggs, he had a notion of how it would feel to have Alex spoon-feed him. Terrifying actually. He didn't want to be in the position he was in, much less be dependent on her for everything.

Then again, perhaps being injured would give him a chance with her. There wasn't another woman in the world he wanted as his wife, experience had taught him that. Trevor's new lady, Adelaide, was beautiful, but Alex, she was priceless for more than her beauty or her gumption. She was intelligent, quick-witted, and she understood the value of hard work. A perfect companion.

"You're not planning on kissing me, are you?" Byron mused.

Brett focused on the old doctor and realized he'd been daydreaming about Alex. "No, I'm sorry. My head feels a bit off. I think I need to get some sleep."

He pulled the covers up with his left hand and closed his eyes.

"Well I guess we're dismissed." Byron exited the room with a chuckle.

"I guess so." Kincaid touched Brett's uninjured shoulder. "I'll come back in the morning to check on you. I put your horse up at the livery."

"Thanks." Brett cracked one eye open. "For everything."

"I expect you'll be home soon." Kincaid walked toward the door. "And Brett?"

"What?"

"You need to work on your wooing skills. I don't think it's her father you want to be kissing." With a smirk, Kincaid disappeared out the door.

Brett cursed himself for mistakes from his past that had caught up to him. He really did want Alex as his bride. What better woman could there be? No emotional tantrums, no silly simpering. She was the woman meant to be his and unmarried to boot.

His mind made up, Brett nodded off to sleep dreaming of ways to convince Alex to marry him.

Cঙৎৎৎৎৎ

"What? You're kidding right?" Alex put her hands on her hips. "You need to stay in my bed."

Brett stared at her until she closed her eyes and her cheeks flushed. He wondered if she hadn't meant to say *my bed*. He'd certainly had dreams of that bed with him in it.

"I mean, stay in the bed here. In the examining room. Listen, Malloy, you were seriously injured. You can't possibly think—"

He put two fingers on her lips. "I think a lot of things. The first of which is to take care of some personal business and I refuse to let you do it for me."

"Ah, okay. I'll get you a chamber pot." She pulled away from his touch.

"No, I want to use the privy." Brett would be adamant about that particular point. She certainly wouldn't be cleaning up his piss if he had any say in it.

"That's foolish. It's upstairs." She waved her hand in the direction of the ceiling. "You can't climb the stairs."

"Yes I can." Brett swung his legs to the edge of the table and paused.

She pushed his knees. "Get back on that bed."

He leaned forward until their faces were inches apart. The sweet smell of her breath tickled his nose. This close he could see the thick eyelashes that graced her beautiful brown eyes. Arousal slid through him like hot molasses. Every moment of time he'd spent with Alex in his arms flew through his memory.

The sweet heat, the delicious pleasure, the seemingly bottomless urge to be with her. All of it washed over him in a wave. Although his head still hurt pretty bad, he pulled her to him. The second their bodies made contact, she hissed—he didn't know if it was in denial or not, but she didn't move away. As he lowered his lips to hers, he forgot all his pains.

She was hot, her lips soft and demanding. After an initial start of surprise, she kissed him back just as fiercely as he kissed her. He tasted her essence, the tang of coffee on her tongue and the sharpness of arousal. He deepened the kiss, his mouth fused over hers, fitting together as if they'd been cast from the same mold.

His body reacted as if set aflame. His cock sprang up like a jack-in-the-box, pressing against his britches and pulsing with need. It had been too long since he'd been with a woman, a lifetime since he'd touched Alex.

The slap was unexpected and did more than make his ears ring. His head now felt like it was going to explode right along with his pants. She looked as shocked as he felt. Her brown eyes widened as she stumbled backwards.

"You kissed me."

"You kissed me back." Brett's pulse pounded through his veins, his head throbbing in tune.

"I did not." She touched her lips and a visible shudder wracked her.

"Yes, you did, Lex."

"Don't you dare call me that." Her face flushed, this time not from embarrassment. Her hand shook as she pointed an accusing finger at him. "You have no right."

Brett slid to his feet, his damn legs almost refusing to hold his weight. He took a step toward her and she took a step back.

"Don't."

"Alex, I... How many times can I say I'm sorry?" He hadn't meant to hurt her. The past should be kept in the past, not dredged up a dozen years later to literally slap him in the face.

"About a million, and even then it won't be enough." She bit her lip and fixed him with a doe-eyed look of hurt. "You broke my heart, Brett. I can't ever forget that."

Brett didn't expect his throat to close up, but it did. Perhaps it was the sheen of tears in her eyes, perhaps it was the aftereffects of the kiss. Perhaps it was the huge thump of his heart letting him know that it wasn't dead.

"Can you ever forgive me?"

She shook her head and left the room, taking Brett's chance with her. He should have tried harder so long ago. She was worth it, yet Brett tucked tail and ran when she'd sent him that letter. Looking back at past mistakes made the here and now that much worse.

Brett should've fought for her back then. Now he'd have to wage war to win her.

Alex sat on the porch and watched the world go by with dry eyes. She couldn't cry any more, but inside, her heart trembled. If only he hadn't kissed her. If only he hadn't reminded her what it felt like to be in his arms, to breathe in his scent and drown in his kisses.

She stayed away as long as she could. It was two hours past dinnertime before she decided she had to go back to feed Brett. Her father was nowhere to be found and because it was a Saturday, there wasn't anyone else around to help.

After slapping together a sandwich for him she stomped in, fully ready to be angry and curt with him. He sat in the chair by the window, looking out into the backyard. His hair stuck up every which way from beneath the bandage, and the shirt her father had lent him lay open, too small to be buttoned.

Brett turned to her and the regret she saw in his eyes stopped her rant before it even began.

"You didn't have to bring me anything. I'm not hungry."

"I don't believe that." She shook herself and walked toward him. No reason to hesitate. Brett had no hold over her.

Liar.

"You need food to heal." She held the plate out to him.

He glanced at the plate and then back up at her. "I hadn't realized you were still hurting."

"Jesus Christ, Brett, just take the food." Her hands trembled with the force of the feelings exploding within her.

"No." He stood, wobbled a bit. "I want you to forgive me."

A million different answers flew through her head, but in the end, her heart overrode them all.

"I can't. You threw me away."

He looked surprised. "I didn't."

Anger roared through Alex and she hurled the plate at him. He grunted as it bounced off his stomach and landed on the floor with a loud bang. The tin rolled away to rest in the corner. The sandwich slid down his stomach and plopped at his feet.

"How dare you! I l-loved you."

Brett frowned. "I never knew that."

Alex put her hands on her hips with a fierce scowl. "What are you talking about? I told you I loved you—you're the one who never returned the sentiment. You're the one who stayed away from me. You're the one who stopped coming by. You're the one who chose work over me." She took a shaky breath and beat back the tears that threatened. "You're the one who told me you didn't think we should get married."

Brett looked as though she'd punched him. Too bad, she couldn't spare a thought for his pain right then. Her own was enough to handle.

She poked him in the chest. "You tossed away what we had and I'll never, ever forgive you for that."

Alex turned to leave the room and Brett grabbed her arm.

"Please, Alex, listen to me—"

"No."

"Dammit." He whirled her around and she slammed into his chest.

His uninjured arm closed around her and she felt a shudder go through him, she wasn't sure if it was from pain or something else entirely. She looked up at him, ready to tear off his hide, but stopped when she caught sight of his gaze whirling with a myriad of emotions. Alex's heart tugged at the most prominent one. Pain.

"I left you alone because that's what you wanted. You told me yourself."

Alex's mouth dropped open. "I did no such thing."

"I never meant to hurt you. I thought you were angry because of all the time I spent at the ranch. You wanted a man who could live in town and be with you. I didn't think I was that man."

Alex knew she had to escape or she'd make a mistake she couldn't afford.

"You were, but you're not anymore." She wiggled in his grasp. "Please let me go. I can't do this anymore."

His hold loosened and she was finally able to take a breath.

"Can we call a truce?"

Alex let out a sigh. Against all her better judgment, she gave in, but only a little. "I'll try."

Brett leaned forward and kissed her forehead. His touch echoed through her.

"Thank you, Lex."

Chapter Six

With some difficulty Brett saddled his horse for the first time since the accident. He grinned in triumph and looked around at the empty livery. On the walk over, he thought a lot about what he'd say to Alex. They'd come to a truce of sorts, and with a little bit more finesse, he might be able to plead his case for marriage.

As long as she didn't hit him again. Brett generally considered his words heavily before using them. Even with all the thinking he'd been doing, he was no closer to knowing exactly what he was going to say. Unusual for Brett, and a very unsettling feeling. One that made his palms itch and his head ache.

Alex had always knocked him somewhat off kilter, now he felt like he was caught up in a twister with nothing to grab onto. He truly hadn't known she was angry with him over what happened so long ago. She'd sent him a letter twelve years ago telling him not to bother her anymore. What else was he supposed to do?

Fight for her. Make her change her mind. Do something besides run.

After catching his breath, he led his horse back to the clinic. When he arrived, Ug greeted him at the door.

"Hey there, boy." He scratched the dog behind the ears and his tail thumped happily on the floor. "Where's your mistress?"

The dog woofed low and padded down the hallway. It was kind of late in the day, she might have already closed up shop while he'd been gone.

"Alex?"

No answer. A tiny sliver of unease slid down his back.

"Alex?"

Ug woofed again and led him to the stairs. Their private quarters were upstairs and he definitely didn't feel comfortable going up there.

"Alex?"

He heard a groan and a thump. Pure energy shot through him as he raced up the stairs three at a time. His head pounded in time with his feet. Ug ran in front of him and skidded to a halt in front of a closed door, then woofed again once.

"Alex?" He pressed his ear to the door. He heard someone crying.

When he turned the knob, it opened easily. The sight that met him was probably one of the most painful things he'd ever seen.

Alex's father Byron lay on the floor in a filthy nightshirt. His grayish pallor stood out against the white of the fabric. His salt and pepper hair stuck up every which way like the end of a broom. Alex had wrapped her arms around his chest and was trying desperately to pull him off the floor.

Her hair swung free and her face twisted in an agonized grimace, tears stood in her eyes. When she saw him, she gasped and one tear slid down her cheek.

Without a word, Brett stepped into the room. Together they pulled old doc Brighton off the floor. He couldn't weigh more than a hundred and forty pounds, likely close to Alex's weight. Not many women could lift a dead weight off the floor close to their own size.

After tucking him in, Alex took a washrag from a basin on the nightstand, wrung it out and wiped down her father's face.

Brett felt awkward and embarrassed for her so he touched the back of her shoulder, then stepped outside the room to give them privacy. He waited for her to come out.

Saying she was embarrassed would be an understatement. To have Brett see her and her father at such a low point wasn't something she wanted to happen. Ever.

Nearly everyone in town knew her father had a drinking problem. It wasn't a secret. Most days you could find him down at the saloon with Mike. Byron was a good man, but her mother's unexpected death ten years ago had sent him over the edge to land in chaos and self-pity. Alex was convinced her father was trying to drink himself to death. He'd lost his spirit when her mother died and never got it back. Regardless of his behavior or his choices, he was still her father and she loved him.

Just as he took care of her when she was young, it was time for her to take care of him. With the amount he was drinking, he probably wouldn't last more than a year. She tried not to think too much about that. She loved him dearly and the thought of not having either of her parents made her heart hiccup and her breath leave her body.

As Alex always did, she focused on the drop instead of the bucket. The smallest amount possible. If she focused on the bucket, she would never get anything done. She considered the drop, the here and now, and knew she had to take care of her father. She cleaned him up as best she could, put him into a clean nightshirt and made him comfortable.

She wiped up the vomit on the floor, picked up all the dirty linens and left her father to sleep. She hadn't expected Brett to be standing there in the hallway. She'd hoped he would be there and at the same time she'd hoped he wouldn't be there. Her heart warred with her head.

Having him assist her with her father...well that was a blessing, but knowing that he saw everything wasn't.

"Brett, I didn't expect you to be up here."

He shuffled his feet and sighed. "I'm sorry. Your dog led me upstairs."

She glanced down at Ug, now sitting peacefully beside Brett's boots. The dog's tongue hung out and he looked at her as if to say, "What? I did the right thing."

"Well, um, thank you for helping. My father's not feeling well and he fell out of bed. I really appreciate you helping me get him back into the bed." She reached out and brushed his wounded shoulder. "Did you hurt yourself?"

"Nah, it's okay. It's healing very well. I had a good doctor."

She smiled weakly and held up the soiled linens. "I need to rinse these out. Can you give me about ten minutes and I'll meet you in the waiting room?"

"Do you want some help?"

"Oh, no, no. That's okay. I can do it." He didn't need to be cleaning up her father's vomit. It was bad enough he could probably smell it.

Brett cleared his throat. "I've had my fair share of experiences with Trevor after a night of drink."

There went the pretense of her father being sick. She'd known, of course, that Brett would figure out what was going on. His brother Trevor did have a tendency to drink quite a bit.

"As much as I appreciate the offer, I'm going to say no. There are certain things I just don't want help with, do you understand?"

"Sure, I understand."

Alex preceded Brett down the stairs, following Ug's wagging tail. When they reached the bottom, he headed for the waiting room and she headed to the kitchen to get out the washtub and put everything to soak in some hot water and soap.

The few minutes that it took her to get the laundry situated gave her the opportunity to compose herself. The embarrassment passed, as did the discomfort. Since it was no secret that her father drank, certainly it was no secret that he suffered the ailments of those who over imbibed.

She twisted her hair up into a bun, belatedly realizing it was hanging to her shoulders. Brett sure did get an eyeful. She ran upstairs and put on a clean blouse, washed her hands again, and then went downstairs to Brett. Taking a deep breath, she strode into the waiting room to face him. Within hours, he'd be gone and her constant state of edginess with him.

He sat with his hat on his lap and sympathy shining in his eyes. "Everything okay?"

"Everything is fine. Why don't we go into the examining room and I'll take a look. I hope you didn't rip out a stitch helping me."

"Nah. It pinched a bit, but it's not bleeding."

That was certainly true. No blood appeared on the light brown shirt he sported. Kincaid must've brought by some clothes. Of course, she had to notice he wore his sinfully tight denims again. The man had nothing else to wear? Even at the emotional low point or perhaps because of it, they caught Alex's attention. She didn't want to contemplate what that meant. Instead, she again focused on being a physician and helping her patient.

When Kincaid had brought Brett in, and she'd taken off his shirt, she didn't pay attention to anything else. It was too important to focus on the wound and saving his life. Being alone with him now was quite different, especially after the kiss.

"I want to recheck it before you leave, just to be sure you didn't re-injure yourself." She walked into the examining room with Brett on her heels.

He sat on the examining table and Alex had difficulty swallowing when he removed his shirt. The expanse of flesh and muscle was a banquet of beauty. She drank it in like a starving woman. The boy's body she had known evolved into an amazingly sexy man. Perfectly formed shoulders, lightly furred chest with whorls of brown hair tapering down toward his belly. She felt embarrassed to note that his bellybutton pressed inward instead of outward. Her finger itched to touch it.

The white bandage on his right shoulder stood out in contrast to the beautiful skin that covered him. She concentrated on untying the bandage without hurting him, twitching when her hands brushed against the hair on his chest.

What was wrong with her? She'd had hundreds and hundreds of patients, probably a thousand in the last ten years. Here she was acting like a complete idiot because it was Brett Malloy on her table. She didn't ever remember having him as a patient before, several of the other Malloys for certain, but never him.

Alex wasn't sure if he noticed her perusal and even if he did, he was too polite to mention it, though he probably should have. A doctor shouldn't be lusting after her patient. She recognized it for what it was—lust. Her past transgressions, or possibly mistakes, catching up with her.

She finally fumbled around enough to get the bandage undone.

"How does it look?" Brett asked.

Alex examined the wound carefully, surprised and pleased at how good it looked. "It looks wonderful, with no sign of infection. You're an amazing healer, Brett."

Her fingertips lightly skimmed his skin. He sucked in a breath. Alex's skin tingled from the contact.

"How long do I keep the bandage on?"

Alex started, a bit chagrined that she'd been daydreaming as she touched his shoulder. "Keep the bandage on a few more days to keep the dirt out. I'll give you more."

"You don't have to do that. We've still got plenty at the ranch."

"I don't want you to use up your supply. You need to have some on hand for anything else that happens." Her mouth twitched, wanting to tease him just a bit. "After all, the roof might attack you again."

"I plan to look up next time."

As Alex wrapped the bandage around his shoulder, she couldn't help but ask, "How is it that you came to be under the wood as it fell off the roof? Mr. Kincaid said he warned you but apparently you didn't hear him."

"Ah." Brett cleared his throat and fidgeted a bit with the shirt in his left hand. "I don't remember. It all happened so fast."

Alex knew a fib when she heard one, but didn't call him on it. He must have had his reasons. As she tied off the bandage, she asked, "Do you need some help putting your shirt on?"

Normally saying that wouldn't have been any kind of issue, but when one brown eyebrow arched at the question, Alex's body heated.

"I think I can handle it."

"Are you sure?" Alex almost didn't recognize her voice, low, a little raspy, and dammit, needy.

Suddenly the urge to feel him, to feel alive, overwhelmed her. At that moment, all she wanted to do was feel something good, no matter if it was right or wrong. Alex decided it was time to start living for herself and her needs. She followed the urge to simply *feel*. Later she'd talk to herself about falling for the same man twice in a lifetime and whether or not it was a good idea. With a deep breath, she threw caution to the wind and jumped in with both feet.

Alex took his face in her hands and lowered her mouth to his. Soft kisses, her lips gently moved against his. Once. Twice. He felt rigid against her, unyielding.

Alex had other ideas. Her tongue swiped his lips, tickling until he opened his mouth. The hot, delicious feeling of kissing him deeply swept through her, raising goose bumps and nipples harder than diamonds.

"Alex," he gasped out between kisses. "What are you doing?"

"Shut up, Malloy." She kissed her way across his jaw to his neck. A moan rose up in her throat as she sucked the salty skin, the arousal building inside her like steam. It needed an escape, a release. It had been so long since she'd had one.

"Make love to me, Brett." It wasn't a question. Before he could protest, she unbuttoned her shirt and took it off, followed quickly by her skirt and chemise. As she stood in her stockings, his eyes drank her in, feasting on her flesh. Alex felt her cheeks redden, but she didn't dare cover herself. This is what she wanted, come hell or high water.

She took his left hand and placed it on her breast. The feeling of the callused palm against her nipple made her gasp. Soon he cupped both her breasts, kneading and tweaking while she continued to kiss him breathless.

"Here?" The one word he was able to get out sounded like a cross between a bark and a groan.

He lowered his mouth to her breast and Alex forgot the question. It didn't matter that the front door wasn't locked. The examining room door was closed and to hell with anyone who interrupted them. She was beyond caring. All she wanted was right there in her arms.

Brett stood and shed the rest of his clothes. His erection stood proud between his legs, larger and hungrier than she expected, and oh so beautiful. She cupped him, loving the feel of satin and steel, and the delightful fur on his balls. Perfectly proportioned, Brett put other men to shame.

"God...Alex...I..." He could barely speak between gasps.

Alex climbed up on the table and spread her legs. "Here. Now."

He stepped closer and when his skin touched hers, she closed her eyes as the euphoria of being naked with Brett overwhelmed her. Then his cock touched her moist pussy.

"Please." Alex couldn't order anymore, she could only ask. The need was so great, she felt like an animal at its basest level with her mate.

His mouth descended to her breast and the tip of his hardness pushed inside her. She bit her lip almost bloody to avoid crying out. So good. So *good*. As he pushed in further, his teeth closed around her nipple and she convulsed, nearly pushed over the edge to orgasm.

Alex reeled herself back in and focused on her breath. Pulling oxygen into her bloodstream, feeling her body stretch to accommodate Brett. Ah, yes, *yes.*

He grasped her hips and thrust forward, as if he couldn't hold back any longer. This time she did cry out. He filled her completely, body and soul. His rhythm was pure Brett, slow and steady. Deeper, then shallow, then deeper again. Designed to drive her mad. She scratched at his back, desperate to keep him within her, making the magic between them that echoed with tingles of pure heat.

"Faster, Brett," she urged, pulling at his firm behind.

"Patience, good doctor." He sucked at her neck, then bit lightly.

"Nope. Not this time." She wrapped her legs around his hips and locked on tight. Embedded deep within her, he pulsed and Alex knew he was close to his release.

She clenched her muscles and rocked. That was all she needed to do. Brett took off like a shooting star, driving into her again and again. She held on for the ride as the lights exploded around her, bringing her to the precipice of pleasure she hadn't experienced in twelve years.

The sky crashed down around her and joy entered her heart. Alex gave herself over and journeyed with Brett to a place only together they could reach.

03࿐80

Stunned. The only word that applied to how Brett felt. Completely stunned. After leaving Alex, he didn't remember mounting his horse or riding down the street. But sure enough, he found himself halfway home and couldn't recall leaving Cheshire.

The fact that Alex had seduced him amazed him. Then the realization that she wasn't angry any longer. Followed by the most intense orgasm of his life. His goddamn knees still shook, not to mention the tightness in his balls. He'd never expected it. Ever. The single fumbling experience with her so long ago hadn't prepared him for this incredible connection. That wasn't a whore's fake enjoyment he'd witnessed. No sir. She'd been as pleasured as he'd been.

Hope bloomed in his chest as elation zipped through him. Perhaps the door had opened enough for him to get his foot in. Alex had always been his perfect match. The twelve years apart had only solidified that. She resided deep within his heart, his soul.

A certain amount of manly pride went with that fact. However, he remembered that he'd just messed around with Alex in her examining room. Naked, sweaty intense sex that he'd be feeling for the next two days.

Goddamn. Where had his head gone? Right to his dick, of course. He could have stopped her. No question there. What man let a respectable woman pull him into bed, or rather her examining table, especially when he's trying to woo her into marriage? Alex was the kind of woman a man married, not fucked. Of course that hadn't stopped him twelve years ago, but then he'd planned on marrying her.

Well, he once again planned on marrying her, didn't he?

Brett shook his head to clear the cobwebs. Time to stop thinking with his dick. Alex messed with his equilibrium too much.

By the time he got back to the Square One it was full dark. A lantern burned in the barn. They hadn't made much of a dent in the repairs on the barn, but the house was starting to shape up although they still needed furniture.

Interesting that there was a light in the barn and not the house. He dismounted some distance away and approached the barn on foot. The night was hotter than usual, with a ghost of the August heat that had roasted the day. He didn't make a sound as he approached the door. He heard the low murmur of voices coming from within.

One of them he recognized as Kincaid, the other unknown. Kincaid and Brett had repaired the door, so he couldn't peer in. Instead, he crept closer and listened, every instinct at the ready.

"We expect you to work. There aren't any lazy asses on this ranch. Is that understood?" Kincaid said, followed by a scrape and a grunt.

"Yessir. I surely do understand that," the other voice replied, a young man by the sound. "I ain't looking for no handout. I told you that. I'm looking for honest work."

Scrape, grunt, thud.

"That's probably about as clean as we're going to get that stall. Shouldn't be too cold tonight. It's warmer than it has been. We don't have any extra blankets."

A shovel thumped on the ground.

"I understand. I got a bedroll. It's done me just fine. It'll keep doing."

"The owner, Mr. Malloy, he should be here soon. I don't expect his business in town will take too much longer."

Brett heard a thread of amusement hidden in Kincaid's words. Dammit. Probably knew exactly what was going to happen between Brett and Alex. It sounded as if a drifter had come by and Kincaid had hired him or at least offered him a place to sleep for the night. Nothing sinister. Something he would have done himself.

Brett opened the barn door. The young man started as if he was going to run, and then stopped himself.

"There you are. Welcome back." Kincaid's right eyebrow arched. "Have a good visit with the doc?"

"Shut up, Kincaid," Brett growled.

Kincaid smothered a chuckle. "Um, this is Mason. He came by today and tried to help himself to some water and some of our food."

Now that was a different story. If he wasn't above thieving, why the hell was Kincaid giving him hospitality? The boy in question was probably in his early teens, filthy hair, but beneath it he looked to be blond. He had brown eyes, and a slight build. His clothes had definitely seen better days. Brown homespun pants topped by what appeared to be a blue shirt, which had long since faded, likely from repeated washings or in his case, no washings. At least not anytime in the last two years.

The boy's gaze constantly scanned around the barn as if he expected some sort of surprise to leap out at him from the shadows.

Brett glanced at Kincaid. "Can I talk to you alone?"

Kincaid nodded. "Set your gear there," he told the boy. "Get settled in. We'll be right back."

The boy's gaze was glued on Brett. When he and Kincaid stepped out of the barn, Brett walked ten feet away before speaking.

"Why the hell did you offer a thief a night in the barn? And it sounded like you were going to hire him?"

Kincaid shrugged. "The only reason he took the food was because he was hungry. If he'd come by when we were here, we would have given him food."

"That doesn't matter. That boy is a thief." Brett didn't want to judge the boy, but anybody taking from him set his slumbering temper off.

"He steals because he has to. Reminds me a lot of me actually. I've been so hungry I've eaten bugs. Been without a home, a family, money. I've been with nothing, nothing but the clothes on my back."

"So you want me to trust this boy because he reminds you of yourself? That's not a very good reason." In fact, Brett didn't like it at all. His hackles stood at attention. Anything out of the ordinary, anything that didn't fit was always suspicious to Brett.

"You want to throw that kid out into the night? Did you look at him? I could practically see through his clothes. That showed me how skinny that boy is. You could count his ribs. I also saw some recent bruises. Now, from what I know of you Malloys, charity and a chance is something you're always willing to give." Kincaid's face filled with remembered anger and desperation.

It went against Brett's better judgment, his instincts, and everything else, but he understood Kincaid's point. Everybody deserved a chance. Even a second chance if the first one didn't work out.

"If he steals anything, I'll have no trouble handing him over to our sheriff, Jim. If he kills me, I'm going to come back and haunt you."

Kincaid chuckled. "Sometimes I think there's a sense of humor underneath all that quiet."

Brett scoffed. "Don't believe it."

Kincaid's grin shone in the darkness. "Just keep telling yourself that. We'll loosen you up eventually."

By the time they stepped back into the barn, the boy had spread his bedroll in the one stall that had been cleaned. Well somewhat cleaned. At least there weren't any holes in the wood, or mouse shit, or raccoons hanging around.

He'd used hay to make a pillow under his bedroll, and hung the lantern on a hook beside the stall door. He'd made it look like a little home. That's when Brett made up his mind— the boy could stay. Brett stood with his hands on his hips looking down at the boy sitting cross-legged on his bedroll.

"House rules, boy. You steal anything, your ass is in the jail in Cheshire. You harm me or mine, you won't see the jail cell. Other than that, I expect you to work, to be respectful and honest."

"Yessir," he responded in a low voice that shook ever so slightly.

Brett stuck out his hand. "Brett Malloy."

"My name's Mason."

As he shook the boy's hand, he realized Kincaid had been right. Nothing but skin and bones.

"Where you hail from, Mason? No last name?"

"No, sir. My mama didn't give me a last name. And I'm from just about everywhere."

"Fair enough, a man's business is his own. Okay then, Mason, did Kincaid feed you?" Brett sure as hell hoped so.

"Yessir, we had some beans, bacon and biscuits. Mighty tasty they were."

"We get up early around here, before the sun, and work hard all day."

The boy nodded, his dark eyes looking like a baby owl's in the gloom of the barn.

"Good night then."

As Brett stepped out of the barn, Kincaid followed.

"Thanks."

Brett turned to look at Kincaid. "No reason to thank me. That boy is going to work his ass off."

Kincaid grinned. "You keep telling yourself that. I'll pretend I don't know any better."

Brett grunted. He was not coddling the boy, he was giving him the opportunity to make his way in the world. Nothing more.

C3ഐ80

A week after her seduction of Brett, Alex saddled Rowdy and headed out to his ranch. She needed to check on his wounds and when time allowed she extended the courtesy of a follow-up visit to her patients at their homes. She could have waited for him to come back into town, and knew she didn't *have* to go see him.

Her physician's side had warred constantly with her woman's side since she'd been with him. Her body, newly reawakened, yearned for his. Her heart kept thumping and sputtering each time she thought of him. While her head told her that she needed to remember he was a patient.

A basket of food hung from her saddle. A patient she'd treated the week before had come by that morning with a complete chicken dinner. A significant amount of chicken and biscuits, and even a peach pie—certainly more than she'd be able to consume by herself. Her father didn't eat much more than a bird, so it was entirely too much food to go to waste.

She knew that Brett and Kincaid would be working hard and they needed to eat. Whatever it was they planned on eating would keep, likely jerky or tins of beans. No need to throw away the fresh food.

Truth was she didn't get a chance to ride her horse as much as she wanted to. Riding was one of the great pleasures in life. She loved the feel of the wind in her face, the power of the horse beneath her. Unlike most women, she didn't ride a mare. She rode a gelding, a big Buckskin that felt like thunder beneath her.

Although she loved to ride, today's expedition wasn't giving her the usual high. Confused, off-balance and needy, Alex rode out to Brett's ranch talking to herself about why she should and shouldn't be seeing him again.

By the time she reached the ranch, the sky was painted orange and pink by the Master's paintbrush. When she rode into the yard, she was surprised to find Brett standing on the porch. He looked as if he'd been dipped in dirt.

"Alex, what are you doing here?"

Alex immediately felt somewhat awkward even though they'd been intimate a week before. Her mouth ran like a mountain stream in spring. "I need to check on your wounds. It's been seven days and I want to be sure no infection has set in." She pointed to the basket. "Plus Sally Jenson came by with a basket full of food to pay me for last week's problem with her son. I set his arm...he broke it climbing a tree. And well, I figured you and Mr. Kincaid would be hungry and tired. I thought perhaps some fried chicken would be welcome for your supper."

When Brett smiled, Alex's heart skipped a beat. She'd been right. He was the most beautiful man God put on the planet.

"Fried chicken sounds just about like heaven right now. That was really kind of you to come check on me, Alex."

When he spoke her name, it was like a caress. Her nipples peaked beneath her shirt. She was grateful her jacket covered the evidence of her desire.

"Let me help you down."

He held up his arms and she frowned.

"You probably shouldn't be lifting something as heavy as me." She glanced at his shoulder. "How are your wounds feeling?"

He flexed his shoulder. "It's a little stiff, but the pain is almost gone. Please, Alex, let me help you down. My mother wouldn't forgive me if you didn't let me be a gentleman."

Against her better judgment, she leaned down into his grasp. As his hands closed around his waist, she closed her eyes.

"Brett." She hadn't realized she'd said the name out loud until he responded.

"Alex?"

Her eyes popped open and she locked gazes with him. A moment frozen in time. She was nearly eye level with him. Unbelievable really. Alex was not a small woman yet he held her suspended at least a foot off the ground. Alex licked her lips while her body ached for him, an arousal that left no part of her untouched.

After Brett's rejection she'd decided that marriage wasn't in the cards for her and had chosen her lovers carefully over the last ten years. There had only been a few and none of them, not one of those four men, had ever inspired the level of heat that licked through her at the mere touch of Brett's hands.

"Am I interrupting something?" Kincaid's amused voice sliced through the moment.

Soon Alex stood on the ground in front of Brett, straightening her jacket and trying to find some semblance of control. She'd been about to invite him to her bedroom. *Stupid, stupid, stupid.*

"I'll just get that basket." Brett turned to retrieve the food from the back of the horse.

Alex's gaze immediately dropped, again, to his trousers. She was pleased to note that he had been as affected by their encounter as she. Her entire body throbbed. A heavy, thick throb as she remembered what he looked like beneath the clothing, and how much she enjoyed the sight, the sounds, the touch.

"Alex brought us a fried chicken dinner."

Kincaid stepped off the porch. "Well that was mighty nice of you, Doc. Did you make it yourself?"

Alex focused on Kincaid, still trying to get her control back. "No, unfortunately my skills in the kitchen are somewhat limited. About the only thing I can make are scrambled eggs."

"Well, you can eat with us then."

"Thank you, Mr. Kincaid. One of my patients brought this huge basket of food as payment. I thought it would be best to serve it to two hungry men who needed it more than I did." Alex was pleased to note her voice didn't shake.

Brett handed the basket to Alex. "We don't have a table yet, but we can spread a blanket on the floor, if that's all right with you."

"That's fine." Did she sound breathless? "Like an indoor picnic."

Brett frowned. "Well, your kindness is most appreciated, Alex. I'm sorry that I can't extend proper hospitality and offer you a chair."

"Oh, that's all right."

"It's not but it will have to be. Well, let me get that blanket for you and Kincaid and I can go wash up."

"Where did you put your medical supplies? I brought some extra bandages with me."

Brett pointed. "I put up a shelf above the sink in the kitchen. Everything is there."

Alex walked in the door and was pleased with the condition of the house. Much better than she'd expected, even if there wasn't any furniture. They'd apparently swept the house, and had put some soap to use. It smelled a bit musty, but it wasn't bad at all. Two bedrolls lay in the living room area. She wondered which one was Brett's, then wanted to smack herself for caring.

A clean spot over on the left beckoned, perfect for their picnic. She set the basket down and went to put the bandages on the shelf. Brett came in with a blanket.

He held it up. "It's clean."

It was a beautiful patterned blanket, looked like his sister-in-law Bonita's work. She was a half-Indian, married to Brett's older brother Ethan, with amazing loom skills. Bonita was a quiet, strong woman who Alex didn't know very well, but what she did know was all good.

"Is this one of Bonita's?"

"Huh?" Brett appeared startled.

"Bonita. Did she make the blanket?"

"Yeah, she did. Um, Ray brought it over with him before."

As they spread the blanket, just the slightest bit of dust flew up.

"There, perfect. Why don't I get the food out while you two wash up." She wanted to touch Brett but didn't and it wasn't just because he was dirty. It was because she needed to regain her self-control, and it wouldn't happen if she touched him again.

"Thank you kindly, Alex." He tipped his hat and left the room, she assumed to wash.

Alex somewhat regretted coming out to the ranch. The reception was odd to say the least. She wondered if Brett lamented their intimacy, or if he burned with the urge to do it again. Funny thing was, Alex felt a little of both herself. Half of her felt a little awkward, the other half wanted to grab him and kiss him.

Brett joined Kincaid at the well pump with a bucket and a bar of soap.

"Water is colder than a well digger's ass." Kincaid had taken off his shirt and left it on the pump handle. "Does the water ever get warmer than this in Wyoming?"

"Not really, these underground streams are fed by the mountains. Always cold."

Brett was startled to find one long scar running from the other man's left shoulder to the side of his waist. Jagged, it had obviously been doctored badly. Brett didn't say a word though. A man's scars were his own business. Besides he was lucky if he could string two words together after his encounter with Alex.

Kincaid had been right. The water was ice cold, but Brett didn't complain. He needed it cold. As it was, he had a half erection from just touching her waist. For a second there, he'd almost kissed her in front of Kincaid. His control had nearly slipped simply because he'd touched her. Madness.

Some soap and fresh shirts transformed Kincaid and Brett into acceptable dinner companions. When they came back into the house, Alex had the food ready.

"We need to set some aside for Mason." Brett sat down.

"Who's Mason?" Alex glanced around.

"A stray," Brett grunted.

Kincaid snickered. "A boy we kind of hired to help us out around here. He just left to go bathe in the creek, after Brett here told him he smelled like a pig."

"What? Brett, that's not nice," Alex scolded with a frown.

"He did smell. I wasn't being mean." He pointed at the food. "Besides I'm the one who said we need to set food aside for him."

"That you did," Kincaid offered. "But if you don't mind, I'll be the keeper of his share."

Brett glared at Kincaid while Alex chuckled. She set out cider for them to drink in tin cups. Kincaid sat right down Indian style and poured himself a cup.

"This here is cider, isn't it?"

"Yes it is. Sally makes the best of everything. I wish I had half the skills she did."

Kincaid took a big gulp and smacked his lips noisily. "This is damn good. Oh, sorry, Doc."

"It's okay. I don't have tender sensibilities. In my line of work I hear a lot worse than damn."

Kincaid grinned. "I'll bet you do."

Alex hadn't been kidding about the food. Sally cooked like an angel. The fried chicken tasted delicious and Brett's stomach purred with pleasure. The biscuits were as good as his mother's and that said a lot. He hadn't realized she'd brought a pie until Alex took it out of the basket.

"Pie too? Woohoo!" Kincaid crowed. "This is the best meal I've had in ages."

"I remembered forks, but I forgot a knife."

Alex dug around in the basket. "Well, I guess we could all just eat out of the pie plate."

"Don't worry, Alex. I've got a knife." Kincaid pulled a lethal-looking blade from the scabbard on his waist. He quickly sliced the pie into six pieces.

Alex nodded her thanks and used a fork to put a piece on each of their plates. The first bite of the peach pie, sweet and sticky, coated Brett's tongue. When he glanced over at her, the expression on her face nearly undid him. She closed her eyes and moaned low, but loud enough for him to hear it.

He didn't realize he was staring until Kincaid kicked him.

"Good pie, ain't it, boss?"

Brett stuck a forkful in his mouth and chewed, almost choking on his desire for the woman in front of him. "Delicious."

Alex's gaze met his and something passed between them. A pulse, a beat, a sweet promise of more than peach pie.

Cʒʅʘʂ

After her examination of his wounds, leaving on just a small dressing, Brett insisted on escorting Alex back to town. It had become full dark while they ate and he was concerned for her safety. Regardless if they were in a small town, a woman traveling alone in the dark was never a good idea.

They rode in comfortable silence. Brett had forgotten Alex was a good horsewoman with an excellent seat. She had a rather large gelding, surprisingly large for a woman. A lot of things about Alex were slightly different from most females he knew.

That included what she did to his equilibrium. He offered her a jacket since the night had gotten cool. Although she already wore one, after ten minutes of riding she finally accepted it. Alex talked about some of the patients she'd had over the last several weeks, then she asked about Brett's family. Alex knew how to keep up the conversation on her own. She was a very positive person, her outlook on life a bright one. Brett had to wonder about that.

Pity Alex's father was a drunk. He'd been forced to give up his practice after a particularly nasty incident with a pregnant woman about a year ago. She'd died in his care, bled to death really, and there were whispers that he'd been drinking during the birth. The baby survived, and Brett always wondered if the woman's husband had. Byron barely survived his wife's death and dealt with it with drink. That drinking likely caused another's death. Alex single-handedly took care of their family, including finances. It had been a blessing she had gotten her physician's license or they might have been out on the street.

Alex's mother had died ten years earlier. Brett didn't blame Byron for turning into a drunk. Many men would have if their wife had died such a painful death from cancer like Mrs. Brighton. Most folks thought men were the stronger ones, but Brett doubted it was true.

Alex's younger brother drowned when she was five. So all in all, Alex's life wasn't a bed of roses, yet she still looked on everything with such a bright disposition. If he hadn't known her better, he would have thought she was touched in the head. However, he did know her, and Alex's outlook on life was one of the reasons he had been drawn to her so long ago.

When they rode up to the clinic, Brett was not happy to note the house was completely dark. That meant old doc Brighton was either passed out or down at the saloon. Either way, Brett was glad he'd brought her home.

They dismounted and Alex took the basket off the back of her saddle. "I need to bring Rowdy down to the livery."

"I'll do it for you."

She peered at him through the gloom. "Are you sure? Will's probably not there."

"I think I can handle putting a horse in a stall and rubbing it down. I've done it a time or two."

"Was that a joke? Were you trying to be funny? Brett, you are loosening up."

"Nah. Just a little bit of sarcasm. Don't get your hopes up."

"I don't necessarily believe you, but I'll let you get away with it for now." She walked up the steps to the porch, her shoes making a dull thump in the darkness.

Their house and clinic sat at the end of the main street in Cheshire. The only folks that usually came down to the end of the street were going to the clinic. Tonight it was deserted, giving the area an abandoned feel.

The only sounds around them were the night creatures. An occasional chirp from a bird or a cricket. They got to the door and he opened it for her, gesturing for her to go inside.

"I want to say thanks again for supper. It was a welcome surprise."

"You're welcome, Brett. I almost didn't come, you know. I don't think it's a good idea for us to—"

He couldn't allow her to finish the sentence, so he tugged her to him and slammed his lips onto hers.

The warmth, no the *heat*, from her mouth seeped into his. After a moment, she softened and moved with him, kissing, nibbling. He tickled her lips with his tongue until she opened her mouth. Her slight, supple tongue gently rasped against his while his hand slid around her back and pulled her close. Dueling tongues, dancing in unison. A small moan came from his throat and echoed through him, making every small hair on his body stand up.

"Alex?" Byron Brighton's voice came from behind them. "Is that you?"

Brett broke free and stepped back, breathing harshly. He tried to speak, but could not. Alex's eyes were full of shock and confusion. It definitely wasn't the time to continue what they'd started, especially considering Byron stood there watching.

Damn.

"Yes, Papa. It's me."

Brett tipped his hat to Alex and stepped off the porch.

"Good evening, Doc."

Byron grunted at him and Alex murmured a good night. Brett still pulsed with arousal and heat, knowing the memory of those stolen moments would haunt his dreams.

Chapter Seven

Brett couldn't believe his awful luck. After arranging to purchase two hundred head of cattle of the mixed Hereford and Longhorn breeds, Casey Beckett gave him the bad news.

"I don't have a bull to go with the cows. Sorry, Brett, but I sold my second bull last fall for some extra money. I can't sell Blue or I'd have no stud come next spring." The older rancher's blue eyes reflected his predicament. He leaned back in the creaky leather chair and regarded Brett across the wooden desk littered with papers and pipe tobacco. He'd arrived at the Circle B to close the deal, and hadn't counted on Casey not having a bull to sell.

A friend of Brett's father, Casey had the second biggest spread in the county. A long, lanky man with jet black hair, he'd spent a great deal of time fighting the elements and ruthless cattlemen trying to claim his land. Casey had hard-won respect and could be counted on for making an honest deal. That was why Brett decided to buy his small herd from him. Brett refused to even consider buying a herd from his father, because he'd take a loss on the sale, no ifs, ands or buts. Brett didn't want his father to have any influence on the financial well-being of the Square One.

He wanted to do it on his own, which meant he needed a bull in the worst way. A herd of cows and steer without a bull to repopulate meant it wouldn't grow and prosper. The calves were the real money for a rancher.

"Do you know of anyone hereabouts who might have one to sell? Pa's got two, but old Brutus can't hardly mount the cows anymore so he needs his young stud, too." Brett gritted his teeth because he knew what the answer would be.

Casey folded his hands together on the desk. "Only one I know of with more than one bull is King Dawson."

Oh, yeah, the news wasn't getting any better.

"That's gonna be a tough buy. King hasn't exactly been a close friend, and he came by the ranch to threaten me a couple weeks ago." Brett ran his hand down his face. "Shit."

"Wish I could tell you better news, but the cattle you're getting from the Circle B is prime stock. Once you get the bull, you should have no trouble growing that herd quick," Casey offered. Not that it would help matters much.

"I know and I appreciate your honest dealings." Brett stood and shook Casey's hand. "Sooner started, sooner finished, right? I'd best get on over to the kingdom and see if I can convince his majesty to sell me a bull."

Casey laughed. "I never knew you were funny, Brett."

That's odd. Neither did Brett, yet Casey was the third person to tell him he was funny. His wit would likely slice a rock in two. Razor sharp and dry as a bone.

CB80B0

Brett tried for days to find another rancher to sell him a bull. No one had anything to offer except a suggestion. King Dawson.

Rumor had it King had at least four bulls, all prime stock too. Casey wasn't the last person to tell him that either. He'd heard it from six different people he'd contacted. Brett didn't relish the thought of doing business with King. Sometimes a fella had to swallow his pride and do what needed to be done. Brett had the will to do just that.

Time to beard the lion.

Brett asked Kincaid to come with him to King's ranch. Leaving Mason in charge felt a little odd, but he did it anyway. The boy looked as if his chest couldn't puff out any higher. Pride did that to a man, no matter what age he was.

"We'll be back shortly so just stay busy cleaning the barn until then," Brett instructed.

He and Kincaid turned their horses toward King's property.

"Yessir. You can count on me." Mason's voice echoed behind them as they galloped away into the afternoon heat. The air had been particularly moist that week, enough that you could almost scoop up a cupful and drink it. Sweat trickled down Brett's hairline and into his shirt. A cool bath would be in order that evening. Preferably with Alex.

Since their encounters, hell, their sweet, hot sex, he'd done nothing but have erotic dreams about her. Shit, half the time he woke up with a dick hard enough to chop wood. Kincaid and Mason were too polite to mention it, but it was no secret. Brett was horny and there wasn't anything he could do about it until he could be with Alex again. Hopefully he could make that happen soon.

He needed to stop thinking about her and concentrate on his biggest problem—acquiring a bull. Brett felt apprehensive about facing King since his entire herd depended on that bull. If King wouldn't sell him one, then he'd have to travel around to find one, easier said than done. Brett would only buy from someone with good stock, a good reputation, and who would guarantee the bull's virility.

A tall order, but Brett had learned how to be a savvy businessman from the best, his father. No way he'd let anyone take advantage of him in any kind of shady deal. That went double for King.

As they rode into the yard, a black dog ran out and barked at the horses. His roan side-stepped the yapping mutt, then tried to kick it.

"Mighty smart horse you got there, Malloy," Kincaid said with a smile in his voice.

"Git on, dog. Git!" The dog kept right on barking regardless of the horse's sharp hooves or Brett's commands. Stupid, stubborn mutt.

King always had a backup plan. Life could kick you in the balls at any time, so King was always prepared. The situation with Brett Malloy and his ranch was just such a reason for a backup plan. He didn't want Malloy anywhere near his ranch, therefore he needed to get rid of him. King had planned on buying Martin's ranch, but since he'd died, it hadn't been a priority. Since Malloy claimed it, the situation had changed drastically.

The fact he hung around Alexandra, well that was the final nail in his coffin. King sat at his polished mahogany desk in his study at the Dawson ranch, gazing at the weaselly looking idiot in front of him.

"So, tell me again what happened between you and your father, Parker?"

With lanky hair flopped over his brow, at least two days' worth of stubble covered his face, and a nose that probably could have used a handkerchief, Parker Samson had all the signs of being a drunk. It had been a lucky break the investigator King hired had even found the man.

The rock he was under had been buried deep, but he'd been found nonetheless. Now King had an ace in his pocket that would get rid of Malloy.

"You understand your father gave his ranch to someone else? A ranch that rightfully belongs to you?"

"Now why did he go do that?"

"My guess is he thought you were dead. It had been at least twenty years since you'd spoken to your father."

Parker shrugged and wiped his nose with one grimy hand. "He don't want me around anymore."

"Is that the truth?" King already knew it wasn't but the little weasel nodded. Old Martin had confessed a lot after a bottle of cheap whiskey, and King had been there to hear it. Not only was Parker a drunk and a weasel, but also a liar—the perfect weapon. "Excellent. Well, I thought maybe we'd take a ride out and visit the ranch. I have two new friends I want Malloy to meet."

Standing in the corner of the room, comfortable in the shadows, stood another one of King's backup plans. The gleam of the man's pistols was the only indication anyone even stood there. He stepped forward into the lamplight.

"Ready to take a ride, Ford?"

The gunslinger's expression didn't change, but he walked toward the door, a determined jingle in his step. King wasn't a superstitious man, but he could swear the spurs sounded like funeral bells tolling. If Brett Malloy was smart, they wouldn't be ringing for him.

The dog barking outside made King smile. Perhaps they wouldn't need to take a ride after all.

King Dawson's house could be considered a mansion by anyone's standard. A huge, sprawling two-story structure with columns in the front, at least twenty glass windows, a porch and a veranda. It had fifteen rooms, including an enormous kitchen for which he'd hired a chef all the way from Paris to cook for him.

Rumor had it he didn't like the Parisian food, and he'd threatened the chef if he didn't start making steak and potatoes. One could dress up a pig, but it was still a pig.

As Brett and Kincaid approached the house, Brett could feel the eyes of King's men watching them. He couldn't see anyone, but the creeping fingers up his back and the hackles standing at attention told him they were there. The damn dog just kept barking.

As they dismounted, Kincaid whistled low under his breath. "A palace for the king?"

"Yeah, and we're in his kingdom so let's step lightly."

"Understood."

As they walked up the stone steps to the house, the door flew open. King stood there with a huge self-satisfied grin on his face.

"Well, well, well. If it isn't my friendly neighbor and his trained dog. How did you put it, Malloy? Get the hell off my land."

Brett contemplated what he should do next when a man walked from the shadows beside the house. A tall, reed-thin fellow with silvery blond hair and nearly colorless eyes. He wore a black flat-brimmed hat, brown shirt and pants. What really caught Brett's attention were the guns, slung low on the man's narrow hips. They weren't the standard Colt peacemakers. He figured they were custom-made, big enough they looked more like cannons.

Kincaid stiffened next to him which answered Brett's question. King had hired himself a gunslinger.

"Got potatoes in your ears, Malloy. I said git."

"I came to do some business, King. Not harass you."

King leaned against the doorjamb. "Business? Now what kind of business do you have with me?"

"I need to buy a bull." Might as well get that out in the open. "Casey tells me you've got four. I'll give you a fair price for one."

King probably couldn't hear Brett over his own laughter. "You want to buy a bull from me? Little old me?"

As if *little* could ever be ascribed to the enormous King Dawson.

"That would be the purpose of the visit."

"Well, your time was wasted. Unless you have about two thousand dollars to give me, the answer is no." The bastard looked so smug, Brett's hand curled into a fist.

Two thousand dollars for a bull? Brett should have known King would be an ass, but asking ten times the price for a bull was beyond even King's machinations.

"Has it got a gold dick, King?"

"Pardon me?"

"I was wondering if the bull had a gold dick, otherwise I can't see spending that kind of money on an animal."

Kincaid lightly touched his arm. Brett's temper had been dormant for so long. Now it appeared it was going to jump out at every spook in his way.

"No, he's not the one around here with a gold dick." King smirked. "Now like I told you, if you ain't got two grand, we ain't doing business."

He glanced at the gunslinger poised next to the porch swing. "Ford here can escort you to your property. Can't you, Ford?"

The gunslinger nodded.

"I think I can find my way home." Brett kept his gaze on the man with the guns. "Thanks anyway."

Brett hated being bested, almost as much as he hated going to see King to ask him for something. It was bad enough to rely on his family for certain things, but to have to deal with a pompous ass like King was hard. Really hard.

"Oh, there's someone I'd like you to meet, Malloy." King gestured to the open door and a stooped, dark-haired man emerged dressed in filthy clothes. He looked like a drunk King had uncovered in an alley somewhere.

"Parker Samson, say hello to Brett Malloy." King gestured toward Brett. "Malloy, meet Parker Samson, old Martin's surviving son."

Son? This was old Martin's son?

Holy shit.

King had just notched up the tension level about a hundredfold. Brett inclined his head toward the stranger, wondering if he really was Martin's son, hoping King couldn't prove it.

"How do I know that's Martin's son? You could've picked up anybody off the streets of Cheyenne and called him whatever you want."

Brett's heart pounded at the implications of a living, breathing heir to the Square One. God help him if he lost it.

"He's come for a visit." King ignored Brett's question. "We'll probably stop on by the old homestead so he can talk about the old days." He smiled like a wolf, all fangs and snarl. "Won't that be nice and cozy?"

"Not especially." Brett wondered what the hell King was up to and what would happen next. Obviously he was busy trying to get Brett off his ranch. Why King would do that Brett didn't know.

"Too bad." King put his hands on his hips. "You're leaving, right? You sure Ford can't, ah, help you home?"

The implication was plain enough, but Brett didn't take the bait. Time to get his ass out of there. Brett tipped his hat at the three men, then backed down the stairs. He decided not to turn around since the gunslinger could easily put a bullet in his back in seconds.

"I'd say stop on by anytime, but that would be a lie," King called. "I'm sure we'll be seeing you real soon anyway."

Brett and Kincaid mounted their horses. They looked at each other and broke into a gallop, riding as fast and as hard as they could, knowing no matter how fast they rode, they couldn't outrun a bullet. King must have been in a generous mood because he didn't have his hired gun shoot them down like dogs.

The ride back to the Square One allowed Brett time to think about what he needed to do to get himself a bull. Unfortunately a specific plan eluded him and frustrated him even more. Brett liked to have a plan, in fact his sanity depended on him having a plan. The added complication of Parker Samson just made matters worse.

Of course his sanity was currently threatened by his obsession with Alex Brighton. Even now, she lurked in the corner of his mind. He swore he could still taste her on his tongue, a sweet, sexy flavor unique to her.

"That wasn't too smart, Malloy," Kincaid said when the Square One came into view.

"What do you mean?"

Kincaid snorted. "Baiting that man like you did. He might be a complete piece of shit, but he hired the coldest and most ruthless gun in Wyoming."

"You know Ford?"

"I know Ford. We've crossed paths a few times, fortunately we've never crossed guns. The man is fast."

Brett knew Kincaid's opinion of the gunslinger was accurate. The man had an air of deadly force around him.

"So what's your suggestion? It seems to me King hired Ford because I hired you. For different reasons of course."

"I know." Kincaid looked out at the horizon, his gaze almost regretful. "Sometimes a body makes choices in life they later regret. What's done is done. I expect my reputation will follow me to my grave, likely dig it for me. Some hotheaded kid who wants to prove he can take down a gunslinger."

Brett hoped it wouldn't happen, but Kincaid's words had the ring of truth to them. It happened quite a bit to men who made their living using their guns.

"What I could suggest is that you get in touch with someone in Cheyenne," Kincaid continued.

"You mean Trevor?" Saying his name was more difficult than Brett had anticipated.

"Maybe, but that wasn't who I thought of. I've got a few friends."

"Really?"

Kincaid's mouth kicked up into a small grin. "I have worked for some reputable people, people with ranches and cattle."

Brett hadn't even considered the possibility, which was a good one. "I really appreciate the help. We can head into town and wire your friends."

By the time they made it into town, Brett regretted the impulse. His mind was full of images of Alex and it distracted him. When they dismounted in front of the post office, which also served as the telegraph office, his gaze strayed south. Toward her.

"Why don't you go visit the doc? You're supposed to get your stitches out tomorrow, right?" Kincaid tied his horse to the hitching post. "One day isn't going to make much of a difference."

Like a siren's song, she beckoned him. The chance to see, touch, feel her overwhelmed him, nearly made him blind. The loss of control frustrated him and he clenched his fists against it. He needed her to ground him, make him feel alive. He needed to marry her.

"Brett?"

"What?" he snapped.

"You're standing there like a fence post. You coming with me or going to see her?" Kincaid's hands bracketed his hips, and in the depths of his eyes, Brett saw a spark of jealousy.

Kincaid envied Brett's relationship with Alex, such as it was, more like an uncontrollable mutual lust. Even now, Brett's buttons felt the pressure of his burgeoning erection.

"I'll meet you back here in half an hour."

With a snort, Kincaid shook his head and walked into the post office, leaving Brett with his thoughts and impulses. He followed the latter and started toward Alex's house. As he walked, Brett picked up speed until he practically ran up the steps.

How the hell did he get to the point where he ran to a woman?

He almost knocked Slim down as he came out the door. In fact, he wrenched his own shoulder trying not to knock the older man to the floor.

"Whoa there, Brett. Where's the fire?"

"Sorry, Slim. I wanted to catch Alex, I mean Doctor Brighton before she finished up for the day."

Oh, now that was a lie and a half.

One silver eyebrow rose. "That so? Well, she's inside taking care of Betty Freeman's little girl."

Damn.

Brett tipped his hat to Slim and went inside to the waiting room. He sat heavily on a chair and ran his hands through his hair. Deep breaths helped him snag control back from the brink of insanity. That's what it felt like anyway. Insanity.

"Brett?"

Alex's voice washed over him and the control he'd tried so hard to grab slipped away again. His head snapped up and he found her standing in the doorway alone.

"Is anyone here with you?"

"No. Betty and Mary just left. I—"

He was on her in seconds. Mouths fused, hot and sweet. Brett cupped her face in his hands and kissed her over and over. The incredible rush of tasting her swept through his body, leaving behind a wake of desire, confusion and desperation.

Alex pressed her body against his, her fingers digging into his back, pulling him closer. The hard nubs of her nipples rubbed against him, inviting his mouth to come by for a visit.

103

"Brett. I can't," she said in between long, fierce kisses. "My...father...is...upstairs."

Shit.

Brett stepped back, breathing hard and shaking harder. He'd nearly fucked her right there in the waiting room with the door unlocked and her father upstairs.

She touched her lips with trembling fingers. "I don't know if I can do this again."

What could he say? Words were never his strength, actions were. He tugged her into his arms and held her tightly. Their matching heartbeats thundered together as the fire of arousal that had to be quenched still ran rampant in their veins. He had missed her and she felt like heaven in his arms.

"Slow down, Brett. You're going to have to give me...time. Would you like to have supper with me? I'm going over to the restaurant. Tonight's meatloaf and mashed potatoes." Her voice sounded husky, strained. No wonder.

"I'm not sure I can sit down yet."

Alex pushed back until she was outside the circle of his arms. The loss of her heat made him shiver.

Her eyes swirled with confusion and arousal. "Please."

Brett reined in his raging desire and accepted her peace offering. "Sure, supper sounds good."

Maybe dinner would give him the opportunity to do some more wooing, or perhaps start wooing. He wasn't sure he could classify what they'd been doing as wooing.

They left her house together, arm in arm, and walked down the street at a much more even pace than Brett had set minutes earlier. A feeling of rightness settled over him, as if being at Alex's side was the place he was meant to be. Sounded silly, but true.

"How do you feel?"

"Good. Better than I expected." Brett hadn't been surprised how quickly his wounds were healing with such an amazing doctor.

"Excellent. After we eat, I'll check your stitches. Save you a trip to town tomorrow."

"Are you flirting with me, Alex? It seems you're just trying to get me to take my shirt off again." He smiled broadly.

"Take it as you wish." She squeezed his arm.

When they arrived at the restaurant, they chatted with several folks having dinner before sitting down. Throughout the meal, Brett had a hard time concentrating on his food. He wouldn't have been able to say if they had meatloaf or chicken to eat. His entire body tingled with the anticipation of being alone with Alex again.

"You keep leaving me behind and I'm going to think you don't like me anymore." Kincaid's voice broke the spell surrounding Brett. He glanced up to find a grinning ex-gunslinger standing beside their table.

"Would you like to join us, Mr. Kincaid?" Alex offered.

"No, that's okay. I ate down at the saloon." Kincaid looked at Brett with an innocent expression. "Should I meet you back at the ranch later?"

Brett resisted the urge to smack the grinning fool. "That'd be fine. I'll be back...later."

Kincaid winked at Alex. She blushed a sweet shade of pink.

"You need anything else?" Brett growled.

"Nope, not a thing. Have a good time, you two." With a tip of his hat, Kincaid left the restaurant.

Brett's good mood nearly went with him. He felt embarrassed to be so wrapped up in a woman, even Alex, he forgot about everything else. Nothing and no one had ever distracted him before.

Until her.

"What is it, Brett?" Alex's brow furrowed in concern.

He shook his head. "I couldn't explain it if I tried."

She smiled crookedly. "You don't need to. I think I understand." After swiping one finger through the gravy on her plate, she opened her mouth, and her finger slid in. Brett forgot to breathe. She sucked the digit, swirling her tongue around the tip. When she pulled her finger out, he wanted to snatch it so he could taste her.

Alex's eyes darkened as her pupils dilated. "I've got something to show you. Will you trust me?"

Brett would've trusted her with his life at that moment. He barely ground out a "Yes."

She left money on the table and stood, placing her breasts eye-level with a very hungry man. Her nipples stood proudly at attention. Brett swallowed with difficulty.

"Come on, cowboy."

Like a mindless idiot, Brett stood, following her out the door. His body throbbed with blazing arousal again. She led him down the street before slipping into an alley. The dark dampness of the space felt cloying, fortunately they arrived at the back door of a building quickly.

"Where are we?"

She shushed him with a hard kiss. "Trust me."

Brett wanted to say he trusted her, but she disappeared through the door of the building. He followed in a blink, his eyes adjusting to the dim light of the lamplit hallway. Alex was just entering a room two doors down. She turned and crooked her finger.

The sounds around him faded to nothing. He vaguely realized they were in the hotel, but he didn't care. All he knew was if he didn't have Alex in his arms in the next ten seconds, he'd need a different pair of britches.

When he entered the room, Alex put a finger to her lips to shush him. She needn't have because he doubted he could speak anyway. He'd been mesmerized completely. The small room was a linen closet. The door shut behind them, the grating of the key in the lock the only sound.

A small window about the size of a block of wood let in weak light, giving an air of mystery and sensuality. The smell of soap and starch wasn't nearly as strong as her scent. He wanted to ask her why they were in the closet but he didn't. A spell wound around them, and one wrong word could break it.

Brett didn't want that to happen. Sneaking into the closet seemed naughty, more than that, forbidden. Something he never expected from Alex. Then again, over the last few weeks she'd done nothing he'd expected her to.

A rectangular table sat in one corner, more than likely where the hotel staff folded most of the linens. Shelves of towels and sheets lined the walls, along with some cleaning supplies like buckets and scrub brushes. And interestingly enough, a chair. A cushioned chair.

With a wicked grin, Alex unbuttoned his shirt, her soft lips kissing each inch of skin she exposed. Brett had never felt so out of control. His entire body buzzed with arousal. He should have told her to stop, but he couldn't. In that closet, they were in their own world and nothing else existed. Just Alex and Brett.

She ran her hands up his chest, lightly scratching his nipples until they were hard points, almost painful. Alex leaned forward and her hot little tongue lapped at one, then the other.

He couldn't stop the shudder that wracked his body. He'd had dreams of Alex's tongue on his body for a very long time.

She slipped his shirt off and laid it on the table. As she lightly touched his back and shoulders, she kissed his healing wound. Brett wondered how long he'd be able to stand. Alex's face pressed against his back and she inhaled deeply.

"You smell good," she whispered.

He didn't think that was too true since he hadn't taken a bath before coming to see her. A quick splash from the well pump had sufficed. However, he wasn't about to argue with her.

Her nimble fingers skimmed along his waistband, reaching around to unfasten his trousers and push them down with his drawers. They puddled at his feet. A sharp pain in his ass made him jump a country mile.

"What are you doing?" he hissed.

"Sorry." She chuckled under her breath. "I couldn't resist."

She'd bitten his ass. Bitten him!

When her touch fell between his thighs, Brett forgot about the bite. With the light caress, he grabbed the table for support. Again she reached around, pressing her breasts into his back. He realized somehow she'd gotten undressed behind him while he was busy acting like an idiot over her.

Her bare skin pushed against him, while one hand cupped his balls and the other encircled his cock. Sweet, sweet heaven.

Her talented hands—he'd dream about those hands for the rest of his life now—pleasured him. Touching, caressing, running her fingernails up and down his sensitive skin.

"Mmmm..." she breathed into his ear. "Someone's ready."

Brett wanted to shout, "Hell, yes I'm ready."

Instead, he nodded, struck mute by her hands on him. She moved away and he felt something pushing against his knees.

As he lost his balance, the chair appeared beneath him and he sat. Thank God for that.

Alex stepped around in front of him. He'd never seen anything as beautiful or sexy as she was at that moment in the dim light of the linen closet. She knelt in front of him and he held his breath, desperate to see what she'd do next.

"What do you want me to do, Brett?" Her hands continued to stroke him, driving him mad. "Tell me." Alex always had shown him what it meant to live in the moment. And he damn sure meant to do it.

He leaned forward to grasp her waist, pulling her to her feet. His tongue snaked out to her bellybutton, licking the soft skin. Looking up at her, he kissed her.

"I want you to ride me."

She smiled like a siren. "That's what I was hoping you'd say."

She straddled him, positioning his aching staff at her hot, wet pussy. She tried to take it slowly, but Brett was done with taking it slowly. His body's needs overwhelmed him. He had to be inside her. Now.

Taking hold of her hips, he thrust upward and embedded himself deeply inside Alex's body. She clenched around him, the heat, the tightness, her musky scent enveloping him, pulling him into a haze of pleasure. He almost spilled his seed immediately.

"Oh, God, Brett. Oh, God," she groaned.

Her breasts sat directly in front of him, within reach of his mouth. He cupped one and glanced up at her while his thumb tweaked the nipple. Her brown eyes were tinged with marked arousal, nearly black with her dilated pupils. A small sheen of perspiration covered her face while her hair hung in tousled waves.

"You're beautiful."

Alex shook her head. "You feel really good."

"This cowboy's ready." He rolled his hips, thrusting upward slightly.

Her gasp echoed through him like rolling thunder. "I can see that."

"So let me feast while you ride. Come on, Lex, honey. Ride."

She slid up until his cock almost left her body, then she slid back down. Hard. Each time she came down, his mouth latched onto a breast. Licking, nibbling, sucking, biting.

Her tempo increased, nearly slamming herself down with each thrust. He was close, so close. His balls tightened, his eyes closed and as he felt her muscles quivering on the edge of release, his world exploded.

Tiny shards of ecstasy pricked him. His fingers dug into her flesh as he held on, trying desperately to ride the wave of pleasure as it washed over him—rocked him to his very core. When it was all over, he realized he'd been holding his breath. He sucked in a huge gulp of air.

"Jesus."

This time not just his knees were shaken. Brett's heart trembled. The world he'd thought he lived in—the world of reality with everything in its place—ceased to exist. What he had instead was the dawning acknowledgement his entire world had just changed and Alex was essential to living. No more pussyfooting around the subject, he needed her.

"Marry me."

CRROSO

King decided to wait and watch from the shadows. Normally watching folks wasn't something he did himself. That's what he paid people for. But this was personal—very personal. So he stood beside the livery and waited. When Brett and Alex left the restaurant, he'd expected them to walk back to her house. What he didn't expect was to see her lead that fool Malloy down an alley next to the hotel. After ten minutes, he knew they weren't coming back out any time soon.

He could have used the word anger to describe what he felt, but it wouldn't have been accurate. What he felt was more like cold fury. A feeling he'd had before, but never as intense as it was at that moment.

When they finally emerged an hour later, he knew for certain what they'd been doing. He didn't have to guess or assume. He knew.

King could almost smell the scent of sex from across the street. Although they were completely dressed, he knew when someone had been fucking. Hair slightly mussed, and her lips, Alex's lips, were swollen. Even in the semi-darkness of twilight, he could tell. They'd been used, and used well.

Alex and Brett were about to find out what it meant to take someone who belonged to King Dawson. A lesson they would not soon forget.

CRANGE

Alex stared at the moon through her window. The sweet night breeze ruffled the gauzy curtains. She'd never felt so confused or lost in her life. Her heart told her Brett was the only man she could ever love. Her head told her to remember how much his rejection had hurt her before.

She hadn't really planned the hotel encounter, but being with him turned her brain off and her body on. She didn't exhibit one iota of self-control where Brett and sex were concerned. The idea of teaching him a lesson, then leaving him unsatisfied turned into something completely different. Alex lost control and left them both shaking from the experience.

When he asked her to marry him, Alex couldn't help the knee-jerk reaction. Slapping him had appeased the vengeful bitch who lived deep inside her—the woman who wanted nothing more than to see Brett get his comeuppance.

There were a million reasons to say yes to his proposal. She could think of one major reason to say no. Brett had broken her heart twelve years earlier and she still hadn't forgiven him. Perhaps it was time to let go of her hurt from the past and embrace the love in the future.

Could she count on him to not break her heart again? To fulfill the promise he made by asking her to marry him? He still hadn't told her he loved her and it made Alex hesitant to believe in them, in their future.

Her love had slumbered for so long, bringing it back to life might be impossible. Alex laid her forehead against the cool glass and sighed. Her breath formed a circle of condensation. She drew a question mark in the moisture with her finger.

What was she going to do about Brett?

Chapter Eight

The August sun beat down on Brett and Kincaid as they worked. Brett figured he could cook an egg on his head, yet they continued to work on the barn. There was so much to do, so much damage to repair. He needed to get the barn fixed and not just for the horses. Grain needed to be stored as winter feed for the cattle. He'd brokered a deal with Casey to include winter feed for the herd Brett had purchased. If he didn't get the barn finished, he'd be knee-deep in hay in the house come wintertime.

His mind kept wandering back to Alex of course. He'd proposed to her and she hadn't answered him. Instead, she slapped him, making his ears ring and his heart ache. He'd thought of little else since then. His need for a bride had taken a left turn and picked up his heart along the way.

With a sigh, he just kept on hammering, telling his heart to shut up for five minutes. If it didn't, Brett might lose his mind. His blisters had long since been covered with more blisters. His hands sweated rivers within the gloves. He'd taken off his shirt, as had Kincaid and Mason. The sun, the heat, were relentless.

"Hello up there!"

Brett stuck his head through a hole in the side of the barn, surprised to hear his mother's voice. He looked down at her standing in front of the barn doors.

"Mama, what are you doing here?"

"Now, Brett, do you understand what it means to be a Malloy? It means we're a family and we're always there when we need each other."

That's when he saw the rest of them. His father, Ray, Lily, Melody, Noah, Tyler, Nicky, Jack, Ethan and Bonita. Jesus, even Nicky's twins were down there. Rebecca appeared to be the only adult Malloy absent. More than likely she'd drawn the short straw for watching the little ones.

They'd come on wagons and on horseback like an invading army. He saw fresh lumber, nails and food. More than that, he saw his family.

Kincaid peeked out. "Jesus, it's a swarm. Should we run?"

Brett punched his arm. "Nah, just my family."

Kincaid's expression closed in on itself. "Great. We could use the help."

His voice was as flat as the sweat-soaked hair on his head. Brett didn't know what Kincaid had against families. Normally Brett would have sent them away and said no. But the fact was, they needed help desperately.

Brett wasn't the kind to ask for it and it was hard to take it when offered. In this case, he'd swallow his pride and his stubborn insistence and accept it. Mason looked like a cornered rabbit in the loft. Brett invited him downstairs.

"Don't worry, kid, it's just my kin. They don't bite. They came to help."

Mason's eyes grew impossibly wide. "You got a big family, boss."

"That's not even all of them. You have no idea."

"There's more?"

"Yep, there's more."

114

Brett went downstairs and introduced everyone to Kincaid and Mason. The twinkle in his mother's eye told him she'd already decided to take on Mason as a pet project. He wouldn't be the first orphan the Malloys had embraced. His sister Nicky and husband Tyler had adopted Noah when he was fifteen.

Everyone set to work seemingly without being told what to do. One thing about the Malloys, they usually worked well together. Brett started unloading lumber off the back of his parents' wagon when Ray joined him.

"I hear tell King went and hired himself a gunslinger." Leave it to Ray to know exactly what was going on.

"Yep, sure did. Name's Ford."

They both grabbed the ends of a stack of boards and headed toward the barn. Ray's gaze reflected worry and a bit of frustration.

"Don't worry about it," Brett said. "I can handle it."

Ray snorted. "With a half-starved boy and a washed-up gunslinger?"

For some reason, Ray disparaging Kincaid and Mason annoyed the hell out of Brett.

"Those are my friends."

Ray inclined his head. "My apologies. I didn't mean to offend."

"I know you didn't."

They set the boards down next to a hammering Ethan and Jack and went back for more.

"With you smack dab in the middle of the boys, I always thought you needed a little extra." Ray grabbed one end of a stack of lumber.

Brett put his hands on his hips and frowned. "What do you mean 'extra'?"

"Are you picking up the wood or are you going to stand there and jaw?"

With a disgusted sigh, Brett picked up the other end of the boards.

"Extra meaning not being the oldest, not the youngest, sort of got forgotten in the shuffle. I never worried about Trevor and Logan—the youngest boys always get the most attention. Jack kept everyone in stitches. Me and Ethan, well, we sort of wrote the book on how to get attention, usually the bad way. But you?" Ray stared off into the distance for a moment as if contemplating his words. "You always seemed a step to the right from the rest of us. I thought maybe you'd outgrow it but you didn't. As if you felt like we excluded you, which isn't true. Not intentionally anyway."

They set that stack of boards by their father and Tyler, then headed back to the wagon for the last stack.

Brett didn't know what to think of Ray's assessment of him. Had he always held himself apart? Was that true?

"But now I'm seeing something different. I hear you're keeping time with Alex again," Ray said as he climbed into the wagon. "She's a good woman, Brett. I never understood why you didn't marry her."

"None of your business." Brett meant that. He didn't intend to discuss his personal, private need for Alex with Ray.

As they picked up the last stack of wood, Ray looked Brett square in the eye. "I just wanted you to know that we're all proud of you, doing this on your own, living out here. You're an independent man and I respect that, but I also want you to know that when you need help, regardless if you ask for it, you're going to get it. You're my brother."

Brett's throat tightened and he found that words deserted him, so he simply nodded and they walked with the last stack of wood toward Kincaid and Mason.

As the work progressed, the rotten boards were tossed in a pile. The women picked them up and stacked them for firewood on the front porch. The men replaced them and moved on. By the end of the day the entire outside of the barn was completed.

Lily and Melody had left a few hours earlier in a carriage. When they came back, they had a wagon covered with a tarp. They each sported big, wide grins. Ray helped his wife and daughter down, giving them both a smacking kiss. His entire family gathered around the wagon and looked at Brett.

"What?"

Jack walked over to the tarp. "I have something for you."

Brett's stomach cramped with the thought of what was under the tarp. He had no idea why he had such a problem accepting gifts, help, or anything from anyone. Made him feel like he truly wasn't meant to be part of the Malloy family. The one person he now seemed able to accept anything from was Alex.

He stepped over to the wagon. "That's a mighty big supper you got there."

Everyone chuckled.

"While it's true you didn't want any help from us, you wanted to do this on your own, we wanted to help when we could. So this is a gift from me and Becky to you." Jack smiled and with a flourish pulled the tarp off the wagon.

Everyone was suddenly silent. Brett gazed at the beautiful furniture he knew his younger brother had made for him. Jack's special skill was wood. Big, small, didn't matter what, he had a gift. He'd made a table and four chairs, the makings for at least two beds, and a parson's bench, along with a bookshelf.

117

Jack pulled out a bundle wrapped in cloth. He opened it up to reveal a handmade wooden sign. He'd carved "Square One Ranch, Brett Malloy, Owner".

"I made this to hang in your new home." Jack handed it to Brett.

Dammit all to hell, Brett felt the prick of tears in his eyes. He hadn't cried in thirty years, which was saying a lot since he was only thirty-three.

Brett took the sign from Jack and then, shocking the hell out of him and his entire family, pulled his brother into a hug. Suddenly there was hugging everywhere and Brett couldn't extract himself, so he endured.

He said thank you again as the furniture was unloaded and brought into the house. He pulled Jack aside.

"You made all that for me in the last month?"

"It was Becky's idea. She's the one who encouraged me to work with wood instead of cattle. Now that I have my own furniture shop, I have all the equipment I need. I even have two people who work for me. And yes, I made it all for you." Jack smiled. The youngest of the Malloy siblings, Jack had the gift of being funny, really funny, and the same bright blue eyes as Brett.

From another wagon, his mother pulled out linens and down-filled mattresses to go on the beds. Brett simply didn't know how to handle so much generosity at once. Fortunately they all seemed to understand and didn't crowd him again.

Mason had stuck to Brett's mother's side like a cocklebur. She invited him over to her ranch to visit any time. The scraggly boy had gained some weight, and had begun to look like a young man. His chest swelled up when Brett's father complimented him on his hammering skills.

As the afternoon turned into evening, they shared a meal of cold chicken and biscuits Lily and Melody had brought. They joked and laughed and sat on the new chairs and bench. Some sat on the floor, but all were comfortable and relaxed.

When his family finally said good night and walked out the door, with the noise that was trademark Malloy, they all headed off to their own houses.

Kincaid had been noticeably quiet during the meal, then absent soon after, but reappeared to say a polite goodbye to everyone. Ray stayed behind. He'd sent Lily and Melody home in the wagon earlier.

"Let me help you get those beds together." Ray never asked, it wasn't his way.

The four of them went inside and made quick work putting the beds together that Jack had crafted. Both beds were in the first bedroom. The second bedroom still held the long narrow bed Brett assumed had belonged to old Martin's sons. He didn't know if Parker was the older or younger one. He didn't want to think about losing his ranch that day, so he pushed the thought aside.

To his surprise, there were linens and a mattress on the bed. Someone had moved Mason's things into the room.

Mason's mouth dropped open. "Is this for me?"

Brett glanced at Ray and they both shook their heads. "Mama."

"My mother has a way of doing what she thinks is right no matter what anyone else thinks. She must not have thought you sleeping in the barn was a good idea. Why don't you go wash up, kiddo, so you can try out your new room."

Brett would have thought he'd offered the boy a million dollars. The young face lit at the simple gesture of having his own room, a bed. His expression was full of awe and hope and what Brett suspected was disbelief.

Kincaid nodded to Ray, then turned to Brett. "I'm going to go settle the horses in the barn." Then he was gone.

"That should be all of it." One of Ray's eyebrows quirked.

"All of what?"

"All of the family's interference. I can come back tomorrow and work on the inside of the barn with you."

Brett forced himself to say thanks, not an easy task. "I really appreciate everything."

"I know and I know how hard it is for you to say that, and accept it." Ray clapped him on the shoulder. "Some days I think Mama picked you up in a cabbage patch."

"Some days I think you're right. Too bad I look just like Pa." Brett grinned.

"You be careful, Brett." Ray's face had the mask of seriousness that was his standard. "In two days a bunch of us are headed to Cheyenne to visit with Trevor and his lady."

That was news to Brett. He definitely wasn't expecting it. "Did he invite you?"

"He invited all of us. I know you've been busy here working hard on your ranch, but I wanted to make sure you knew you were invited. We're only going for the day."

Brett shook his head. "No, I'll stay here."

"Suit yourself. Good night then."

After Ray left, Brett stood alone in the house, gazing at the new furniture. The scent of fresh cedar and oak filled the room. If nothing else, this reminded Brett he wasn't alone in the world, that his family loved him, and it made life worth living.

A thought niggled at the back of his mind and try as he might, he couldn't dislodge it. Alex. The one person he'd like to share the moment with wasn't there.

CRSOBO

In the morning, he couldn't wait any longer. Brett got up before the sun and headed to town. The humid air weighed down on his skin and he felt rivulets of sweat slide down his back. He barely noticed. His focus was on getting to Alex. He had to see her, to make her believe he wanted to marry her.

Her reaction to his marriage proposal alarmed him. Brett had no idea how much the pain was still embedded in her from so long ago. The last thing he wanted to do was hurt her again, but he was determined she'd be his wife. Come hell or high water.

When he got to the clinic, he found old doc Brighton alone reading the newspaper with a cup of coffee. Brett stepped into the room, disappointment warring with discomfort over seeing the older man again.

"Mornin', Byron."

Doctor Brighton looked up from the paper, and his gaze scanned Brett with something like distrust, which surprised him. Unless the doctor knew what he and Alex had been up to.

"What are you doing here, Brett?"

"I came by to see Alex. Is she here?" He fiddled with his hat, feeling like the young man who had shaken in his boots at the thought of facing his lover's father.

"No, she had to go out and see a patient."

"Do you know when she'll be back?"

Byron set the paper down and scowled. "Are you keeping time with my daughter again?"

Brett opened his mouth then closed it. "I'm not sure."

"If you hurt her, you'll have me to answer to. I might be old but I can still kick your ass."

Brett was hurt by the implication. "Hurt her? I'm not planning on doing anything but marry her."

"Marry her? Why the hell would she marry you? You've got nothing for her." Byron snorted. "Except a run-down ranch with no cattle."

"I'm picking up my cattle tomorrow and the ranch will make a profit. I guarantee it." He was more than determined that his dreams would come true, regardless of what anyone else thought. Byron's reaction knocked him a bit sideways—the doctor had never been anything but polite.

"If she tells you no, you walk away." The newspaper shook in Byron's hands.

Brett knew he had to tread lightly or risk his entire future because Alex's father disapproved.

"Sometimes the heart does the speaking for the head. If Alex really doesn't want to marry me, I'll let her go. I'm kinda hoping she will though." He plunked his hat on his head. "Could you tell her I stopped by?"

Byron glared at him until Brett nodded and left the room. The thick morning air did nothing to alleviate the bad feelings churning up inside him. What if the older man did something to ruin his chances with Alex? He wouldn't do that, would he?

CROSS

The crickets sang their nightly lullaby in the sweet warm air. It had to be close to midnight. Alex sat on the front porch staring off into the starry sky, thinking of Brett. It had been almost a week since she'd seen him. Her body craved not just his touch, but his wry sense of humor, the rare smile and his solid presence beside her.

Ug lay on the porch next to her, his snout hanging over the edge of the first step. She reached down to scratch him behind the ears and he woofed softly.

"At least I know you won't leave me, will you, Ug?"

He woofed again as if he understood her. One good thing about a dog, they were loyal. She didn't have to worry about what he was thinking or feeling. His tail and tongue told her all she needed to know.

"Alex?" Her father opened the screened door and poked his head out. "What are you doing out here so late?"

He'd promised Alex he'd stop drinking and he hadn't a drop since that awful day when Brett had to help her with her father. It had been a really rough time for him, for both of them. Times of craving and misery, and sleepless nights. Alex tried to assist as best she could, but it was a personal battle her father had to fight on his own.

"Just relaxing, Papa. Are you going to come out and join me?"

He looked left then right before stepping out. In his day, Dr. Brighton had been an extremely handsome man. Blond-headed like Alex, with dark brown eyes, an easy smile and broad shoulders. He'd been quite the catch.

Now his blond hair was mostly gray, and reflected the need for a good brushing and likely a good washing. He wore a robe, a nightshirt and a pair of slippers, and in his hands he clutched a pipe. It had been the last Christmas gift he'd received from his

123

wife. Since he'd given up drinking, the pipe had been a constant companion.

He shuffled over and sat beside Ug on the porch step. Alex figured the dog had filled a void in her father's life since he'd been sober. She knew Ug was a smart dog; she was convinced he was also a compassionate one that understood when humans were in need or in pain.

Her father petted the dog's mismatched fur. Alex swore she heard the dog sigh in contentment.

"Pretty night," her father said.

"Yes, it sure is."

"We're due for some rain soon I think. My knees have been bothering me the last couple of days."

Alex murmured an appropriate response, unable to be drawn into simple conversation. Her mind and heart were so tangled up, small talk seemed impossible. Not a good thing for a doctor whose patient rapport pretty much depended on her ability to talk.

"Is this about Brett Malloy?"

Alex started as if he'd pinched her. "Excuse me?"

"I might be a drunk, but I know he's been in the house and I know you've been mooning over him since you were just a young girl."

"I-I, that is..." Her cheeks heated as she stumbled over her words. She was glad for the cover of darkness so her father couldn't see her. It was one thing to seduce a man, it was another thing if her father knew about it. "Yes, he's been around. He was injured, um, out at his new ranch a few weeks ago. So he's been in for treatment."

"Uh-huh, you keep sticking to that story, sweetheart. It appears to me you've been spending an awful lot of time by yourself, thinking."

Alex sighed and wrapped her arms around her knees. "I have been thinking a lot about him. You're right."

"What are you going to do about him?" Her father was like a dog with a bone.

She playfully smacked his arm. "You're awfully pushy tonight, Papa. I've loved Brett all my life, even though I wanted to hate him since he, well, since we were together years ago. But now, I'm beginning to doubt myself."

Her father lit his pipe, the glow of the match bright in the darkness around them. "How so?"

"I don't know if I can explain it, but I feel adrift. Like I lost my rudder somewhere and I can't seem to steer straight." Alex didn't know up from down anymore. Loving Brett Malloy had always been a difficult proposition. After her last encounter with Brett, he hadn't come to see her once, perhaps because she'd slapped him after he asked her to marry him. Had she made a mistake?

"Be sure you know what you're doing, honey. He hasn't got much to offer you."

Brett didn't have anything to offer her but himself, and when he had, she'd thrown it in his face. Her hurt and anger had overwhelmed the love that still beat for Brett inside her. It was time she and Brett had a long, honest talk. The next time she saw him, she'd tell him exactly how she felt.

"Thank you, Papa. You've been very helpful, as always."

She leaned over and kissed his whiskered cheek, glad the only scent surrounding him was the smell of tobacco.

"You're welcome."

They sat on the porch for a while longer, enjoying each other's company, the companionship of Ug and the symphony the night creatures played for them.

When Alex headed upstairs for bed, butterflies danced in her stomach. She had a feeling her life was about to take an unexpected turn.

CRITICAL

The dew still coated the grass as Brett and Kincaid rode over to Casey's ranch to pick up the herd. Nothing compared to the thought of having his own cattle on his ranch. It felt amazing. In fact, Brett almost felt a smile playing around his lips at the thought. Kincaid must have seen it.

"Don't get all mushy on me, Malloy. You'll ruin your reputation."

"Shut up, Kincaid."

Kincaid chuckled as they continued riding. It was a beautiful morning before the heat of the day truly hit. Even some of the stickiness was gone as if Mother Nature knew it was an important day. When they got to the Circle B Ranch, Casey met them on the front porch of the house with a big grin.

"You're early, Brett."

Brett tipped his hat back and tried to remain casual. "Well, I figured we could get the work done early and both be onto the rest of the work for the day."

"Uh-huh. Okay. Let's get you that cattle." Casey called two of his men over, Slim and Poke. "They're gonna help you drive the herd over to your property."

The four men headed out to Casey's north pasture to cull the two hundred head from the herd, which wasn't hard work.

They were fat, happy cows and docile steers. Casey had rich grazing land and plenty of it.

Soon they had the small herd together and were driving them toward the Square One. Brett made Kincaid ride drag. Kind of a mean thing to do, but the best way to learn how to drive a herd of cattle was to ride drag. Brett would just offer to heat the water for baths later because he'd surely need to scrape the dirt off.

Moving the cattle only took an hour, an hour that Brett would treasure. In those sixty minutes, he became a cattle owner. *Finally.* The docile cattle moved well, with few strays. Brett was glad he'd purchased Casey's cattle. It had definitely been the right decision as they were obviously good stock. Who knew what King's cattle would be like? Probably as ornery and difficult as their owner. The men finally reached the grazing land of the Square One. The creek sat on the east side of it, only a short distance from the property line of the Dawson ranch.

The grass was thick and sweet and the water constantly flowed no matter the rainfall amount. The creek itself was fed by the mountains so it was cool and crisp water, perfect for his new herd. He thanked Slim and Poke who headed back to Casey's ranch. Kincaid rode up slowly, a sour expression on his dirty face. The filth coated him from his hat to his boots.

Brett tried to look innocent. "What did you think of your first cattle drive?"

"I'd rather have a tooth yanked."

"I think you did great. We didn't lose any cattle and we hardly had any strays off the path."

Kincaid swiped a hand down his face and glared at the dirt on his hand. "So this is why I was at the back, huh?"

Brett shrugged. "The greenhorns always ride drag."

"Well thank you very much, Mr. Malloy. I'm gonna go take advantage of that creek over there."

Brett gestured widely with his arms. "Feel free."

As Kincaid rode toward the water to get clean, Brett gazed out over his herd, his cattle, and felt a sense of pride he'd never had before. Almost made him want to write a letter to Trevor to say thank you. If he and Trevor hadn't gotten in that fight, Brett probably would have never decided to move to the Square One. Funny how life changed so quickly. One never knew what was around the next corner.

Brett made sure the cattle were settled and taught the basics to Mason and Kincaid on what to do. Although it wasn't necessary, they decided to spend the first two days keeping watch twenty-four hours to make sure the cattle were settled comfortably. After that, with the abundance of grass and water, the cattle were not likely to wander far without provocation.

They would just need to check on them every four to six hours, and with only a fifteen-minute ride from the house and barn, it would be an easy job. One Kincaid and Mason could handle even if they didn't have much cowboy experience. He needed to brand the cattle; unfortunately his brand hadn't come in yet. Keeping a close count was important as well.

Mason couldn't count so the job fell to Kincaid and Brett to monitor the number in the herd. When Brett finally made it back to his bed at the Square One, he was beyond exhausted. It was a good exhaustion, the sweetest sense of tired he'd ever felt. As he lay in his new bed he thought about all that had happened over the last month and he realized life had given him his chance with the ranch.

He was grabbing onto that chance with both hands and wasn't about to let go for anyone or anything. He'd fight King and whoever Parker Samson was. The ranch belonged to Brett.

The next best thing would be to have someone to share it with. Brett fell asleep with Alex's image dancing behind his eyes.

CƳƧƠƀƆ

Alex hadn't meant to eavesdrop. She and Ug had walked to the post office to fetch the mail as they did each day. It was early on a beautiful summer morning and the feel of the sun on her face was invigorating. As they walked down the wood-planked sidewalk, Ug stopped and sniffed something every few moments, then happily bounded after her with his tail wagging. She smiled at his antics.

Something caught Ug's attention because her faithful pooch bolted toward an alleyway between the general store and the post office.

"Ug, come back here."

The dog chose not to listen to her. Alex glanced around but no heroes were to be found. She was alone on the street. With a sigh, she headed into the gloomy space filled with crates. The smell of urine and vomit assaulted her nose and she pulled a handkerchief out to press it to her face. What in the world had happened here?

"I'm telling you, this is the plan. You do it or I'll shove you back under that rock you were living under so hard you'll never come out again." The harsh whisper from behind a large stack of crates made Alex stop in her tracks.

"I don't got no money to pay for a lawyer," came a whiny reply.

"I'll pay for the lawyer, you piece of shit. You just stick to your story, got it?" A thump and a groan alerted Alex to the fact that more than just a conversation was happening. Someone was getting thrashed.

Fingers of dread marched up her spine at the hate and vehemence in the reply. The deeper voice was oddly familiar, but because of the whisper, it was hard to identify.

Suddenly she heard a bark and Ug raced toward her.

"What the hell was that? Someone's listening."

Alex picked up the edge of her skirt and ran, heart pounding and the sharp taste of fear on her tongue. The sunny street seemed miles away and she wondered how she'd walked so far into the alley without noticing.

"Get her!"

Only a few more feet and she'd be free. Ug ran by her side, a comforting presence in a terrifying moment. Just as she reached for freedom, a hard yank on her hair pulled her up short and back into the darkness of the alley. Pain radiated through her head as she was dragged back down the narrow passage in the dirt.

When he finally stopped, a thin, weaselly looking face loomed over hers. "She's a pretty one, eh? I'll teach her to listen to other people's talk."

Ug barked, growling and snapping as she tried desperately to push the man off her. A sharp fist to her jaw filled her mouth with blood as stars swirled in her vision. His weight pushed down on her chest.

She could only wonder what these men would do to her as a hand closed around her throat. Ug growled again then was cut off abruptly. Alex pushed and shoved as hard as she could but soon blackness enveloped her.

Her last conscious thought was of Brett.

Brett help me. Oh God I need you.

Chapter Nine

Brett woke up before the sun, his heart and stomach jittery. It had been a long week since he'd seen Alex, but it was more than that. He needed to see her, touch her.

He missed her. Him, loner Brett, the Malloy who didn't seem to need anyone. He wasn't ready to figure out why, although one day he'd have to. As he rode into town, his mind filled with images of Alex in everything from a dress to nothing at all. His pants grew tight at the images dancing through his brain and he had to tuck them away or risk being the laughingstock of Cheshire.

He arrived in town around nine in the morning. The street bustled with wagons. He tipped his hat to a cowboy he knew as he tied off Rusty at the hitching post in front of the post office. After he went inside and posted a letter for Kincaid, he heard a faint whine that sounded like a dog.

He stood there for a few moments, but it didn't happen again. As he put his foot in the stirrup, he heard the whine again from the alley. He sighed and ran a hand down his face. His mama always taught him to help those in need, even those of the four-legged variety.

Brett tied Rusty off again and walked toward the alley between the post office and the store.

"Hello?" He peered into the gloom, but didn't see much of anything. A small scraping sound tickled his ears, followed by the whine again. He fished a match out of his pocket and struck it on the building beside him.

After his eyes adjusted to the small flame, he spotted the dog dragging itself down the alley with bloody fur and what appeared to be a few missing teeth.

Brett kneeled down slowly, careful not to startle the poor thing. When he got closer, he recognized the dog as Ug. The match burned his fingers and he cursed, dropping it.

Sweet Jesus.

Alex's dog was near death in an alley. He reached out his hand and the dog sniffed it carefully. He gave a few half-hearted licks.

"Good boy. Now let me get you home to your mistress so she can fix you up." Brett gently scooped the dog into his arms. He walked out to the street. As he lifted the dog up onto Rusty, canine teeth closed on his biceps. "Ouch. What are you doing, Ug? I'm trying to rescue you."

The dog whined again, this time louder, followed by a short, painful howl.

"What is it? Is it Alex?"

The dog woofed and licked its bloody nose.

Brett's entire body snapped tight. Alex must be in the alley, maybe injured like Ug, or possibly... Nope, not even finishing that thought. His practical side took over and forced him to quell the panic that rose like a tidal wave inside him. He lay the dog down on the sidewalk.

"You stay right here with my horse, Ug. I'll be right back."

The dog whined and his dark eyes seemed to bore right through Brett. He took off running down the alley, lighting a match as he went. He cursed when the first one snuffed out because he was moving too fast. Taking a deep, calming breath, Brett lit his last match and stepped further into the alley.

"Alex?"

The only sounds he could hear were coming from the store's loading dock. The alley was dead silent. He stepped further in, his nose wrinkling at the rancid smell. The Goodsons really needed to clean out this area. His foot connected with something soft and sheer dread blossomed in his stomach. The match went out.

Brett knelt down, arms outstretched in the shadows and found a warm body. Oh God, oh God. He'd recognize her scent anywhere, even in a dim alley surrounded by the scent of shit and piss.

"Lex, honey, I'm here." His voice cracked on the last word.

When he touched her face, he felt the soft puff of breath on his skin. Sweet relief flowed from the realization she was alive. In what condition, he had no idea. As if handling a precious doll, he lifted her in his arms. She was boneless, seemingly lifeless, but he knew better. He felt her heart beating against him and thanked God over and over for that damn dog Ug.

When he reached the end of the alley, he didn't want to look at her, but he knew he had to. Blood covered the right side of her face and her neck was swollen and purpled with bruises. Her shirt was ripped open, the tender skin beneath scored with more bruises and scratches.

Absolute fury overtook him at what had been done to her, which was better than bawling like a baby, his second impulse. Now he knew how Trevor felt when Adelaide had been shot. Love, it seemed, turned a man into a mass of emotional havoc.

Peter Goodson came out of the store. "Brett? What happened?"

"Someone beat the hell out of Doctor Brighton. I need to get her over to her clinic right now. Can you hold her while I mount the horse?"

"Of course. My God, look at her."

Brett didn't want to, but his eyes couldn't seem to look away. He placed Ug in front of the saddle then mounted and gestured for Peter. The older man lifted Alex up into his arms.

"Do you want me to get the sheriff?"

"Yes. Send him over to the Brightons. I only hope Byron is ready to treat his own daughter."

Brett rode as quickly, but as gently, as he could. He didn't want to jar either one of them any more than necessary, but the ten-minute slow walk seemed to take ten hours. Her blood dripped onto his shirt and pants, and the swelling in her neck seemed to grow each second.

He finally arrived at the Brighton's house, his worry making him mad with the sensation he should be doing something for her.

"Byron!" he shouted at the top of his lungs. "Byron!"

Old Doc Brighton came hustling out of the house, a napkin tucked under his chin and crumbs on his lips. When he caught sight of Alex, his face drained of all color. He stumbled toward the horse.

"What happened?"

"Somebody beat her and damned near strangled her. Can you handle her weight while I dismount?"

The older man nodded, tears standing in his eyes as he took his daughter into his arms. Brett jumped off the horse and took her from her frail-looking father.

"Take Ug inside too."

Byron nodded and spoke softly to the dog as he lifted him up and they walked into the clinic. Brett headed for the examining room with Byron on his heels. As he laid Alex down on the table, the old doctor found a comfortable blanket in the corner for the dog.

"You wait here until I can get to you, boy." He scratched the dog's lopsided ears with trembling hands.

"Have you been drinking?" Brett asked before he could think twice about it.

Byron's gaze narrowed. "Haven't had a drop in almost a month. I wouldn't treat my daughter if I wasn't sober."

That was good enough for Brett. "What can I do?"

"Go get some hot water from the reserve on the stove, and wash your hands thoroughly."

The old doctor must have had some medical spark left in him because he went to work immediately on his daughter. He'd seen Alex work before, but never her father. Byron had precision and skill. Brett nearly danced in place, waiting, hoping for something to do. When Sheriff Jim Weissman showed up, he gratefully went to speak to him.

Jim had been friends with the Malloy brothers growing up and still attended family gatherings. A fair man, he'd been sheriff for more than eight years in Cheshire, a good lawman the town was lucky to have. His brown eyes were full of concern as he sat with Brett in the waiting room.

"Brett, what the hell happened?"

"I have no idea. I had just gotten there to mail a letter when I heard the dog. Then I found her and God, I don't remember. I just got here as fast as I could." His hands shook as the full weight of what happened to Alex hit him like a hammer blow. If he hadn't heard Ug, hadn't been there at that precise moment, she might have died.

His stomach cramped and his breakfast threatened to make a reappearance. God, life was too short to waste time. As soon as she woke up, he'd tell her how he felt and ask her to marry him again. This time he wouldn't take no for an answer.

"Did you see anybody?"

He'd almost forgotten Jim was there. "No, I didn't see anyone near the alley. I did see Poke from Casey's ranch as he was leaving the store with an armful of stuff."

Jim nodded. "That's what Peter Goodson told me too. A regular morning."

"Who would hurt her, Jim?" Brett knew his friend wouldn't have the answer but he needed to ask it anyway.

Jim put his hand on Brett's shoulder. "I don't know, but I'm damn sure going to find out."

"Brett?" Byron called from the doorway. He had bloodstains on his shirt and perspiration dotted his forehead. "She's sleeping comfortably. No broken bones, but she lost some blood, a hunk of her hair. Fortunately there doesn't seem to be any permanent damage to her neck."

"Thank God." Brett inhaled and exhaled slowly, telling his racing heart to calm down.

"I'm going to take care of Ug now."

"You give that dog steak for the rest of his life, Byron." Brett stood. "He saved Alex's life."

Byron's eyebrows went up. "I always knew he was a smart dog."

"Can I see her?"

"Yes, but please don't wake her. She needs to rest."

Brett nodded and headed for the examining room, desperate to see her, to touch her. He stepped in and was pleased to see Byron had washed the blood from her skin. She

136

lay beneath a blanket. Her blonde hair lay lifeless on the pillow, while her face, her beautiful face, was swollen and bruised.

His breath hitched and for the second time in as many weeks, tears pricked his eyes. No man had call to beat a woman half to death. His thirst for revenge was nearly as strong as his need to be near her. Brett touched her cheek, careful to avoid any scratches or bruises. He leaned down and kissed her forehead, shocked when a drop of moisture landed on her pale skin.

"You get better now, Lex. I've got a lot to say to you."

Byron came in and gently picked up the dog. "I'll take care of Ug in the kitchen."

Brett nodded. "Thank you."

"No need to thank me, she's all I've got." Byron left Brett and Alex alone again.

"Me, too," Brett whispered. With one last brush of his lips against her forehead, he left her to sleep.

Time to go hunting.

CRANGE

Brett left with Jim to go examine the alley where Alex had been attacked. They didn't find much except for a piece of cloth and some shoe prints. As they walked out of the alley, Brett kept his gaze on the ground searching for something. Anything that would help.

"You boys lose something?"

King's booming voice echoed through the entrance to the alley. Brett turned an angry gaze to the pompous ass.

"Alex almost lost her life here today. Know anything about that?"

Instead of shock, King appeared bored with the topic. "You know how these modern women think they can do whatever they want. Sometimes it catches up with them."

Brett didn't even realize he'd moved until Jim grabbed his arm.

"Easy there, Malloy."

"Maybe now Alexandra will realize she needs to marry me after all."

"When hell freezes over," Brett growled.

"Funny, Malloy. I believe the icicles are forming down there as we speak." King grinned. "It's you I was looking for actually. I have some papers for you."

He held a sheaf of folded papers toward Brett who snatched them.

"Make sure you read that carefully, Brett. You might even want to find yourself a lawyer." With a tip of his hat, King walked down the street.

King's words rang like a warning knell to Brett. It had something to do with Parker Samson and the Square One. None of that mattered at the moment since Alex was first and foremost on his mind. He stuffed the papers in his back pocket and continued his search with Jim.

After two more hours of speaking to folks and examining every nook and cranny in the alley, they had to concede no one saw or heard anything. Nor was there any evidence of who had beaten Alex. Frustrated, Brett headed back to the Brighton's house. He needed to see her one more time before going home to the Square One.

As he rode up, he found Byron sitting on the front porch smoking a pipe, looking like he'd been rode hard and put up wet. The older man's face drooped with exhaustion and his eyes reflected deep sorrow.

"Doc? What's wrong?"

"I'm not sure Ug will make it. I wasn't able to get to him for an hour and he's lost so much blood..." He gestured in the air. "I've done what I can but I'm no animal doctor."

"We need to put him in the room with Alex."

"Why?"

Brett didn't know exactly what was between Alex and Ug, but it was a deep bond. "She and Ug are connected somehow. He saved her life today and now she can save his by being close."

"He's in the kitchen in a basket, resting by the stove."

Brett nodded and went into the house to fetch the dog. His furry body was wrapped in bandages, but clean of all blood. Half of one ear was missing. Poor dog. Brave little thing. He picked up the basket and the dog let loose a small whine.

"It's okay, boy. I'm just bringing you to your mistress."

As he walked into the examining room, Alex's scent washed over him. He breathed deeply, bringing part of her into his body. It had an amazing calming effect on the nerves stretched taut over the day's events. She slept on, breathing evenly. Brett set the basket next to the cot and he swore the dog looked more peaceful.

He leaned down and pressed his cheek to hers. The warmth of her skin penetrated his and for the first time since finding her, he felt like she'd be fine. Now if only he could say the same for himself. He sat with Alex for hours, simply holding her hand.

Brett didn't know if she even knew he was there, but it didn't matter if she did or not. He was there because he needed to be. It had to be close to midnight before Brett decided to head home. Kincaid and Mason were too green to be left alone for more than a day. The ranch was his and he had to spend at least half his time there, even if his heart stayed with the woman before him.

"I'll be back tomorrow, honey. You get better."

With one last kiss on her forehead and a pat on Ug's head, Brett left to go home. He passed Byron on the steps.

"Send someone to the Square One if you need me, Byron. It's old Martin's ranch."

"Thank you, Brett. After what I've done, what I've said..." Byron shook his head. "I can't say thank you enough for saving her."

Brett blew out an unsteady breath. "I didn't save her. You and Ug did. I was the lucky fool who happened to be nearby."

Byron's eyes narrowed. "Have a care. I have a feeling this is only the beginning of what's to come."

Brett had the same feeling. The air around them seemed charged with a brewing storm.

Chapter Ten

When Brett finally made it home, he was exhausted. A bone-deep weariness seemed to permeate every part of him. He saw Kincaid's horse in the barn as he unsaddled Rusty, however Kincaid was nowhere to be seen.

Brett's feet dragged on the way to the house. The day had sapped him completely. When he opened the door, the smell of chili and cornbread washed over him. His stomach woke up with a vengeance, snarling like a rabid dog. He realized he hadn't eaten since breakfast. The whole situation with Alex had made everything else seem unimportant.

The empty house welcomed him home. His home. He tossed the papers King had given him on the table and headed for the stove. More than likely his mother had come by with the food. She was already looking out for Mason, and he and Kincaid reaped the benefits.

After spooning some chili into a bowl, he snagged three pieces of cornbread and sat at the table. With only the sound of the crickets for company, Brett ate his dinner and tried not to think too hard. Thinking brought him around to Alex and that led to a twisted up gut.

Instead, he wiped his mind clean and focused on filling his belly. After the food disappeared, his exhaustion crept back. Brett laid his head down on the table.

It seemed as though he'd just closed his eyes when the crinkling of paper woke him. He cracked one eye to see Kincaid sitting across the table from him with one leg resting on the corner of the wood. The ex-gunslinger had a handful of paper and frowned as he read.

"What are you reading?" Brett mumbled sleepily.

Kincaid's gaze snapped to his. "I don't know. You left it on the table."

Brett hadn't even bothered reading them. "What does it say?"

Kincaid glanced down at the papers. "Apparently Parker Samson is challenging your right to ownership of this ranch."

The words dropped like stones in Brett's stomach. "Son of a bitch. I knew King would try to take the Square One."

Kincaid handed Brett the papers. "Yep, you got it. The paper is signed by Parker Samson, only surviving child of Martin Samson."

Old Martin's son. Maybe. King better have serious proof the man was who he said he was. All Brett had was the deed signed over by Martin. Brett had no bill of sale of course, because he won it in a poker game. He could not lose the Square One to anybody.

No way in hell he'd let that happen. Not without the battle of his life.

"Fucking King Dawson and his meddling goddamn fingers."

Kincaid nodded. "Nobody else has the money or the balls to do it."

That was the gospel truth. King had to have whatever toys he wanted, regardless of who he stepped on with his huge feet to get them.

Brett tried to read the papers in front of him, but everything blurred together at the very real threat just leveled at him. He couldn't lose the Square One. Not after everything he'd done in the last several weeks to make it into a home. Hell, Kincaid and Mason had become his family and he had a herd to consider.

He didn't have a lot of money, but every cent Brett had would go toward a lawyer to fight the bastard. He didn't care how much money King Dawson threw, Brett Malloy would not go down without a fight.

CRORED

Alex woke up slowly, pulling herself from a slumber as deep as a canyon. She felt like she'd been sleeping for years, her lethargy was so great. In a flash, she remembered the men in the alley. The last thing she could recall was the skinny man with the greasy hair pawing at her shirt. Then everything went gray.

By the smell, she could tell she was in the examining room. She reached up and touched her throat, not surprised to find swelling and extreme tenderness. The bastard had choked her. She didn't know why she was still alive, but she thanked whatever angel had looked out for her.

"Alex?" Her father's voice broke the silence around her.

She opened her eyes a crack to find him hovering over her, looking for all the world like a harried father. With bags under his eyes, and hair sticking straight up, he could have scared patients. The concern in his eyes told her all she needed to know about her condition after the brutal attack.

"H-how..." She tried to speak but her voice was a croak.

"Brett found you. Ug called to him and your cowboy rescued both of you." Her father cupped her cheek. "I can't tell you how grateful I am to him."

"Ug hurt?" she managed to say.

"Yes, he was hurt pretty badly but he's hanging in there. Brett put his basket in here next to you. Seems to be good for both of you."

She reached down and encountered warm fur and bandages. Thank God he was alive. She was sure the dog had tried to protect her and ended up being injured for his efforts. Alex had never had a dog before and now understood why people loved them so much.

"Good dog," she whispered as she stroked his fur. A soft woof sounded.

"You've been unconscious since yesterday. Ah, Brett stayed by your side till past midnight. He said he'd be back today to see you. Couldn't convince him to stay away if I tried." Byron closed his eyes. "I was wrong about him, sweetheart."

She frowned. "What do you mean?"

"I did something a long time ago that hurt you. I was only trying to protect you, but instead it soured your view on love. I'm sorry for that." He stroked her hair. "You deserve a second chance with him."

"Wh-what do you mean? What did you do?"

"It's not important." He shook his head. "Just make sure you keep an open mind, Alex. I think he really does love you."

What exactly did her father do? Was he the reason the relationship with Brett went sour before? From the look on her father's face, she didn't think she'd get an answer from him.

Her father seemed to shake himself out of the melancholy that gripped him. "Nothing broken, but I think your right shoulder is sprained, too many contusions to count, some scratching, and your throat of course. Another thirty seconds of choking you and he w-would have killed y-you." Her father's face crumpled and he buried his face in his hands, sobbing quietly.

"Oh, Papa." She touched his silver hair and thanked God she still had those she loved around her. Alex tried to smile, but the left side of her face hurt too much to do so.

Alex hoped Brett would come sooner rather than later. With her father's blurry confession, the urge to speak to Brett grew stronger with each passing moment.

CR&R&

Brett spent half the night worrying about his ranch and the other half worrying about Alex. He didn't sleep other than the brief nap he'd taken sitting at the table which Kincaid had interrupted. Brett was damn glad he had, too.

He considered himself an intelligent man, but the legal jargon confused the hell out of him. He needed to go talk to the lawyer in town, Tim Green. Until he realized the very last page of the documents had Tim's name on them, which meant he was working for King Dawson.

That left Brett with no choice—he had to talk to another lawyer. The closest town was Hawk's Bend and last he heard they didn't have a lawyer, but he'd wire over there and ask the telegraph operator. If anybody knew what was going on it would be Jake, the man who ran the post office and the telegraph from a small storefront. At least that was a decision made. One decision. He felt like he had a million to go.

He was just pouring coffee into a cup when Kincaid emerged from the bedroom, freshly shaven with nary a hair out of place.

"You look like shit," Kincaid mused.

Brett scowled. "You know, you do work for me. You should be a little more respectful."

Kincaid laughed.

"Yeah, I know I look like shit. I didn't get any sleep," Brett snapped.

"That's obvious."

Brett's scowl deepened. "I feel like somebody who doesn't know how to swim and just jumped into a deep lake."

Kincaid slapped him on the shoulder. "I do have some good news. I heard from a friend of mine yesterday, Asa Keenan. He has a bull he'd be willing to sell you. He's got a ranch just outside Cheyenne. He'll give you a fair price for it too. If you trust me, I can broker the deal for you."

Brett trusted Kincaid and buying a bull would likely take every dollar he had. Well, what the hell. If he lost the ranch, at least he could take the cattle with him. They'd merge nicely into his father's herd.

"I have to hire a couple wranglers to help out."

"Why don't you ask your family for help?"

He'd actually considered that. However, Brett wanted to do this by himself, to not ask them for any more help than he'd already been given. It was important to him to achieve his dream.

"No, I want to do this on my own."

Kincaid slammed the coffeepot down on the stove. "You know, I hope you don't mind me saying this, but it just fires me up to see you like this. You have got a family most people would kill for. Hell, they came and rebuilt your fucking barn for you. Brought you furniture and food and everything else, then left. I've never had anyone that I could count on for that, much less family. You act like they're a pain in the ass. Let me tell you something, Malloy, that's one hundred percent shit."

Kincaid grabbed a piece of leftover cornbread from the warming pan on the stove, then snatched his cup and stalked out the door, slamming it behind him so hard, the coffeepot rattled.

Brett saw Mason peeking his head around the corner. "Are y'all fightin'?"

"No. Kincaid was just busy kicking my ass."

Brett knew Kincaid was right. He did have a family he could count on who loved him. A bit of shame crept in and settled on his heart. He had a first-class family and it was time he started treating them like one. He'd go over and talk to Ray and then go into town to telegraph Jake in Hawk's Bend, and send one to his sister Nicky to see if they could spare Noah for a little while. Then he'd go see Alex.

Before the day was over, Brett would stand up and be proud to carry the name Malloy.

He finished off his breakfast and went outside to find Kincaid. Brett had given him time to cool off before going to look for him. If there's one thing Brett had learned about the ex-gunslinger, he needed his time to himself. Brett understood that all to well, since he was the same way.

He found Kincaid in the barn fixing a stirrup. Kincaid glanced up, his dark eyes as flat and unreadable as a winter sky.

"You're right. I'm an ass. I'm going to ask my family for help and I'm going to stop complaining and treating them like they don't deserve to be treated." It wasn't easy for Brett to say it out loud, but after he'd done it, he felt better.

Kincaid inclined his head and continued to work on the stirrup.

"I'm going into town today to take care of business and see Alex. I'll get that money so you can contact your friend Asa in Cheyenne."

"Sure thing, boss."

Brett saddled his horse, listening to Kincaid murmur to himself. Brett couldn't make out what he was saying, but more than likely he was grousing about Brett's stupidity.

"So you and the lady doctor, huh? Are you going to go see her again?"

Brett's stomach knotted. Kincaid had no idea what had happened to Alex the day before.

"I'm going to see her because someone beat the hell out of her yesterday and then choked her. The only reason she's alive is that crazy dog Ug."

Kincaid dropped the tool and the stirrup, straightening. His hands drifted to the pistols that never left his hips.

"Who?"

"I don't know who. The sheriff and I looked for hours yesterday and couldn't find anything."

Kincaid's mouth tightened. "You find out who, you let me take care of it for you."

The vehemence in Kincaid's voice surprised Brett. "Have you got a crush on my dear lady doctor?"

"No. She's the first woman to treat me like a man instead of a pair of guns attached to a body. She was kind to me. Alex is a good woman. Anyone who does that to someone who means something to me deals with my kind of vengeance."

148

Brett didn't know exactly what kind of vengeance Kincaid had in mind. He was glad Kincaid was on his side though. He pitied the poor fool after both of them got through with him.

CB&CBO

The noon mealtime arrived as Brett finished what he needed to do in town. He stopped at the restaurant to pick up food for three and headed to Alex's house. Cognizant others would be watching, Brett forced himself to a slow walk on Rusty. He tipped his hat and was polite when needed, knowing all he wanted to do was break into a hard gallop.

It seemed like weeks had passed since he'd seen her, although it had been less than a day. Byron would have sent word if anything bad had happened. Brett arrived with the expectation that Alex had survived the night without incident. Any other possibility wasn't entertained.

He dismounted and secured his horse, then carried the basket of food toward the house. A sign on the door made him run the last ten feet. At first, his eyes refused to focus. He finally read the small scrawling script which had to belong to Byron.

Unless it's a life-threatening emergency, please come back in three days. Drs. Brighton.

Brett knocked on the door with shaking hands. He breathed in and out slowly, pulling air into his body and pushing out the stupid panic that had grabbed hold. When no one answered his knock, his patience ran out. Brett opened the door and walked into the house.

"Byron? Alex?"

He heard what sounded like a kitten mewling, otherwise the only other sound was a clock ticking somewhere. The lack of noise didn't concern him as much as the mewling. He set the basket of food down and crept up the stairs toward the sound. When he reached the landing, he paused to get his bearings, then continued on.

The keening noise came from within Byron's room, the door open. Brett sidled closer and peeked around the doorframe. The old doc sat on his floor, a bottle of cheap whiskey in one hand, a handkerchief in the other. The thought that he sat upstairs while his daughter struggled for life angered Brett beyond belief. He wasn't about to consider the possibility Byron was drowning his grief.

"What the hell are you doing?"

Byron started and scrabbled to the left. "Who is that?"

Brett stepped into the room. "It's Brett Malloy, Byron. I repeat, what the hell are you doing?"

The old man turned watery brown eyes up at him. "I almost lost her."

Dropping to his knees, Brett yanked the whiskey out of the doctor's hand. "So you thought it would be a good idea to pickle your brain? What if she needs you?"

Byron waved his hand in the air. "She's fine now. B-but I almost l-lost her."

Brett stood and looked down at the older man with something like pity. "I won't pretend to know what you've gone through, but I can tell you that you're hurting her by getting drunk. If she needs a doctor, you need to be sober."

Covering his face with his hands, Byron wept. Brett hoped like hell he'd never be such a mess over anyone. He'd like to think he was stronger than that, both mentally and emotionally. Another reason not to drink too much.

150

"I sent you that letter."

Brett froze on his way out of the room. "What did you say?"

Byron took in a shaky breath. "The letter from Alex when she told you she couldn't be with a man who loved cows more than her. It was me."

Squatting down, Brett looked the older man in the eye. "Why?"

"You were a cowboy, a nothing with no prospects other than what your daddy gave to you. Alex was brilliant, on her way to being one of the first female physicians in the country. She spent half her time mooning over you. I couldn't let her throw away her future."

The words hit like hammer blows. He didn't know whether to be angry or insulted, so he decided on both.

"You didn't do anybody any favors by meddling, Doc. I hope to hell you've learned your lesson. You cost us twelve years of our lives apart. I just hope she can forgive you."

He stood and left the doctor to his misery before he said something he'd truly regret. Brett took the whiskey downstairs and dumped the booze down the kitchen sink. Relieved that Alex had survived the night, he finally went in search of her. After Byron's confession, there seemed to be so much he needed to say, enough that his heart was near to bursting.

The examining room door was closed, and he opened it without knocking. Alex sat on the cot with a book in her hands. Ug lay beside her. Both of them were covered in bandages and had obviously seen better days. Bruises and cuts decorated the left side of Alex's face. Her lips were swollen and split, but the sight of her neck made his breath catch. Large, ugly oval-shaped marks clearly outlined the fingers that had tried to squeeze the life from her.

The fury zipped through him, leaving him shaking and confused. Alex had turned his life upside down in less than a month. He wondered what he'd do if he ever lost her and he hadn't even told her he loved her.

He loved her.

It wasn't the best time in the world to realize his feelings for Alex, particularly since she glanced up at that exact moment and spotted him. Vulnerable, Brett's voice ran away as his mouth seemed to be stuffed with cotton.

"Brett." She sounded like she'd been shouting all day, but he knew it was due to the bastard who choked her. Alex set the book down and did an imitation of a smile, then grimaced. "I keep forgetting I can't do that."

Brett stood there, probably looking like an idiot. She frowned and sat up straighter.

"I'm glad you came by, Brett. I...I need to talk to you. First let me say thank you for saving me, Brett. Papa told me." She fiddled with the book.

"It wasn't me. It was this mutt of yours." Brett finally found his voice again as he touched Ug's head. "I think he might even be smarter than me."

Alex scratched Ug behind the ear. "He's a treasure all right. Papa did a good job fixing him up, too. As far as I can tell, he's just weak."

Ug managed a soft woof.

"It's been a long time since we went our separate ways. We never talked about what happened. With everything that's happened"—she flapped her hand in the air—"I think we need to."

When her brown gaze met his, his heart dropped to his feet.

He fell to his knees next to the cot and took her hands. "I...I'm not very good with words, Alex." His voice sounded creaky and unused. No surprise there.

"There's no need to be. Just listen to what I have to say." She blew out a shaky breath. "When you sent me that letter...you broke my heart. If only you'd come and talked to me, but you didn't. You took the coward's way out and it made me furious."

Brett should be surprised, but wasn't. Perhaps Byron's meddling also included a letter to Alex. "I didn't send you any letter."

She frowned. "Yes you did. You told me we didn't suit and there was no reason for us to ever get married."

"Alex, I never did such a thing. I'm the one who got a letter." He opened his wallet and pulled out a yellowed, faded paper that he'd kept with him for years.

Alex reached for it with shaking hands. She opened it up and read the words Brett could recite by heart.

Dear Brett,

I've decided that we have no future together. Your place is with cattle, mine is with patients. Please understand that I hold you in the highest regard, but we can no longer see each other.

Alex Brighton

Alex folded the letter and handed it back to him. "I didn't write this."

Brett's heart thumped hard. "I didn't write you a letter either."

She looked stricken. "Brett, who could have done this?"

"It doesn't matter now." He couldn't possibly tell her about Byron. "The last month has been the most exciting, frustrating and amazing of my life. That's due in part to the Square One,

153

but mostly...it's you." He didn't remember the room being so hot.

"Do you have something to tell me?" She looked hopeful and scared, exactly how he felt.

"Alex, I'm never going to be a poet. I, uh, can't seem to stop tripping over my own tongue." He laughed nervously.

"That's okay, Brett, I don't think I fell in love with a poet."

Love.

He hadn't expected the word to come out of her mouth. Brett wiped his forehead and concentrated on finishing what he'd set out to do that morning. He looked her in the eye and focused on seeing her face every day.

"I figure I'm not good enough for a doctor, but for some reason God don't agree with me. He made me fall for you and made my life a living hell when we're apart." It all came out in a rush, like someone had pushed the air from his lungs. "I know we messed up the first time around. I messed up, I should've come to you after I got that letter. I'm hoping you'll give me a second chance."

"Brett, what are you trying to say?" Her eyes gleamed with unshed tears.

"Not that you have to say yes, but I'd really like you and me to get married. I know I ain't perfect, and I have some bad habits, but I promise you I will be the best husband I can be."

There, he'd said it. Not with any eloquence and maybe not even coherently, but at least he got it said.

"Did you just ask me to marry you again?"

"Yes, I did and you know it. Stop torturing me, Lex." He cupped the right side of her face, careful to steer clear of the tender spots. "I don't think I could get any more nervous if I tried... Please, Lex." He swallowed the lump that jumped into his throat. "I need you."

She kissed his hand. "You haven't been an easy man to love."

Love.

"I know."

"Do you have anything else to say?"

Love.

"I do, but you'll have to be patient with me." Telling her he loved her would take time. Brett hoped like hell she understood because he didn't. The words stuck in his throat like a corncob, refusing to budge no matter how he tried to yank them out. She wanted love, he was sure of it. He could give it to her, all of it, but apparently he couldn't say it.

"Promise me you'll talk to me more? No silences?"

"I can't say it'll be an easy promise, but I'll do my damnedest to keep it." His lungs ceased to function and spots danced in front of his eyes, as he waited for the woman who owned his heart.

Alex kissed his cheek. "Yes."

"Yes?"

"My answer to your question. Yes, I'll marry you."

Brett's heart skipped a beat. At first he thought he'd heard her wrong, but nope, he hadn't. Not only had he asked Alex to marry him, but she'd said yes.

She'd said yes.

"Well, hell, I...I thank you."

"You're welcome." Alex glanced down at her lap. "Brett, I'm glad you asked again. I wasn't sure of how I felt. Today I promised myself we'd be honest with each other."

Brett took her small hand in his. "Do you think we have a chance?"

"I think we do. I didn't earlier, but I do now." She tried to smile, then winced.

He leaned over and gently kissed her bruised cheek. "You ready to be strong with me, Lex? It isn't going to be an easy road for us."

"I'm ready as long as we can continue, ah, testing our physical relationship for a bit longer."

Brett chuckled. Yep, she was his Alex.

Yes, love.

CRWECBO

Noah arrived two days later riding his favorite horse Ringer, a rather strange-looking mustang with a white ring around its neck. Noah had captured Ringer in the wild and tamed him. No one but Noah had been able to ride him.

When he rode up to the ranch, Brett had just finished fixing the corral fence post that had fallen victim to Mason's roping practice. After Noah dismounted and walked toward the corral, Brett was surprised to notice Noah was taller. The brown-haired skinny kid had matured into a full-grown man in a matter of a few years. When did that happen?

"Noah. Thanks for coming to help out." He took off his gloves and shook Noah's hand. A firm grip and huge hands. Yep, Noah had definitely crossed the line from boy to man.

"Happy to. Ma's been hinting it's time I took the foreman's job, but I've got other plans."

Brett cocked one eyebrow. "Care to share what those plans are?"

"Not today, but one day I will," Noah said with a grin.

Of all of Nicky's brothers, Brett had taken a shine to the skinny orphan she'd adopted. He'd been the first to take Noah hunting and to teach him how to prepare game for eating. Not only that, but Noah was quiet, unlike Nicky who was a chatterbox of the highest caliber.

Kincaid stepped from the barn and greeted Noah. "Hey, welcome to the ranch, kid."

Noah smiled. "Glad to be here. The twins and Frankie can be like a constant cyclone."

"I've met the twins so I can agree with the cyclone idea. Do I want to know who Frankie is?"

Shaking his head, Noah laughed. "My youngest sister. She's just a baby."

"God, there's more kids?" Kincaid looked horrified.

"Oh yeah. You didn't even meet Jack and Rebecca's." Brett elbowed Noah. "We Malloys know how to make babies."

Noah blushed and chuckled nervously. "Thank God I'm not truly a Malloy."

Brett let loose a hoot, glad to have a little bit of humor back in his life. It was good to have some light amongst so much darkness. He settled Noah in with Mason. The younger boy gazed at Noah with something like hero worship when he found out Noah had been an orphan too. A great deal passed between them with only a glance. Brett was doubly glad Noah had come.

The next week passed quickly with Alex making enormous strides in her healing progress and Brett trying to figure a way to keep his ranch. He found a lawyer in Hawk's Bend named Matt Jamison, a young man who had just graduated law school. He hadn't even had his first case yet. Brett, however, had no choice but to hire him. His next option was to go to

Cheyenne and find a lawyer. Unless he was desperate, a trip to Cheyenne was not going to happen.

Noah pitched in right away and the Square One was running more smoothly within days. Tyler had taught him every smidge of information about running a ranch and it showed. Brett had no idea why Noah didn't want to be foreman of the Bounty ranch and he wouldn't pry. Obviously Noah could run it without question.

Brett spent most of his days on the ranch, teaching Mason and Kincaid what he could, then he spent his evenings in town with Alex. Although a good hour one way, the daily trip was as necessary as breathing. They had told only their parents they were getting married. Byron seemed relieved, and Brett's parents whooped with joy. They'd always liked Alex.

Until the ranch was truly his without any legal challenges, the plans for a wedding had to wait. Alex understood that and didn't push for anything other than his time. Brett wondered what took him so damn long to realize how amazing she was.

When he'd told her about King finding old Martin's son and filing a claim on the ranch, she almost had smoke coming out of her ears. Brett had to keep her home by distracting her with kisses. She seemed bound and determined to go kick King's ass and he loved her for it.

Life should be perfect, but a constant dark cloud hung over the Square One. Brett wanted the fight over quickly because a long legal battle would destroy him.

Chapter Eleven

Alex dressed quietly, carrying her shoes down the stairs so as not to waken her father. She didn't want him to know she was going out for the first time in ten days. The beautiful summer sunshine called to her and a mission of utmost importance beckoned.

She was going to talk some sense into King Dawson whether he liked it or not. Furious that he'd dug up some fool claiming to be old Martin's son and was threatening Brett, she wouldn't let the behemoth get away with ruining her future husband's life.

She'd worn a high-collared dress to hide the yellowed bruises and dabbed rice powder on her face. No one would ever know she'd been injured. It was the first time she felt truly anxious to be back into her normal routine, but there were a few things she had to take care of first. Like King. She had to be the first person to tell King about the engagement. God forbid he heard it somewhere else first.

She walked down the sidewalk toward the livery. Will hooked up a buggy to her horse Rowdy since riding wasn't a good idea yet. Within ten minutes she was on her way out to the Dawson ranch. The wind felt marvelous on her face, the smell of the summer abundance heavenly.

Beth Williamson

Birds twittered, squirrels chattered, and the day couldn't be more beautiful. Alex's heart was lighter than it had been for weeks. It would all work out, it had to.

When the main gate to King's ranch came into view, an armed sentry let her pass without comment. Just the thought that he had someone with a rifle guarding the gate made her stomach jumpy. Who was he protecting himself from? As she pulled the buggy up to the house, King appeared from the barn, a thin man dressed in black and a pair of guns followed behind him.

"Alexandra! This is a surprise."

"Why is that, King?"

"Well, just... I mean I heard... I usually visit you. I'm pleased you came to me." His lascivious words were punctuated with a matching grin.

Her skin crawled with revulsion. Lord help the woman who fell into King's marital trap for the third time.

"I didn't come to *you* exactly. I came to speak to you about something." She glanced at the man standing ten feet behind him. "Can you ask your friend to leave us alone?"

King's eyebrows shot up. "Ford, take a walk." He spoke without even looking behind him. The spooky man disappeared back into the barn.

Alex felt a bit better without the dark man's eyes boring into her. For some reason, just the sight of him made her nervous.

"I came to ask you to leave Brett and the Square One alone. I don't know who this man is claiming to be Martin's son, but the fact that you are pushing this legal battle is shameful. I thought you were a good person, King. I don't want to change my opinion." She sat up straight, speaking from her heart, hoping he'd reconsider his involvement.

160

King leaned against the side of the buggy. "Well, now, I have a vested interest in who my neighbors are. Malloys have been known to take land that didn't belong to them."

"That's a bald-faced lie and you know it. The Malloys don't steal."

He shrugged. "Not how I hear it. Trevor cheats at poker, too. They're a shifty bunch for sure. I am making sure the good folks of Cheshire have upstanding citizens for landowners."

Alex couldn't believe the nonsense coming out of King's mouth. "That's the biggest pack of lies I've heard in years. You know that's not true."

"I know it is true. You need to send that Malloy pup on his way and think about our future together on this ranch. Those two hundred head of his aren't going to give him two nickels to rub together." He leaned forward and touched her knee.

She removed his hand deliberately and with aplomb. "I will not send Brett on his way, nor will I ever marry you, King. I told you that hundreds of times. Now let me tell you something new. I am marrying Brett so I will be your neighbor soon on the Square One. I won't take too kindly to someone trying to force us off our land."

"You're marrying that bastard?" His voice echoed like a rifle shot around the yard. A dog barked and chickens squawked.

"Yes, I am. Now please give up this legal battle and your quest for my hand in marriage. Neither one of them will bring you happiness or prosperity. I'm asking as a friend." Alex felt like she was speaking a different language than King. He didn't understand a word of it.

"Not on your life. Be prepared, Alexandra, this fight's gonna get dirty and bloody. If you want to live I suggest you rethink your decision to marry that piece of shit."

Now that was a threat. Alex hated being threatened—the typical way of bullies. Bullies couldn't be tolerated.

"No, you listen to me, King Dawson. You are not a monarch but you're certainly a tyrant. Like a little boy denied a sweet, every time something is taken from you or not given to you, you pout and throw a tantrum. The citizens of Cheshire have had enough childish antics. For once in your life, grow up and be a man."

She snapped the reins and pulled away from him. Alex felt a smidge of glee when he almost fell on his head and surely swallowed a mouthful of dust. King called her name, but she simply kept driving until she left the main area of the ranch.

The glee quickly turned to serious contemplation. Obviously King was twisted enough to do whatever he had to do to get Brett off the Square One and marry her. She had to speak to Brett about what to do if royalty came calling with guns.

King stared after the buggy until even its dust cloud disappeared into the horizon. He barely controlled the urge to mount his horse and teach her a lesson in manners. That little bitch dared insult him and his manhood. Never mind the rest of the shit she'd spouted, her parting comment about him felt like a bucketful of hot coals.

Burning, sizzling heat scored him from head to foot. He heard Ford walk up behind him.

"Time to get serious with Malloy. Make sure he knows living next to me can be dangerous."

"I'll be sure the message is loud and clear." Ford's raspy voice almost sounded pleasured.

As King struggled to maintain his temper, Ford rode away on his gray gelding. Alexandra would regret her visit to the Dawson ranch by nightfall.

CRESO

Mason had the makings of an excellent ranch hand. As he practiced lassoing a docile cow, the loop landed straight and true. Mason jumped off the back of the paint Brett had borrowed from his father and hurriedly took the rope off.

"How was that, boss?"

"Not bad. Another four hundred practice throws and you might be ready." Brett couldn't believe he was teasing the boy.

He could tell Mason wanted to complain or gripe, but didn't. Instead he just said, "Yessir," and climbed back up on the sturdy horse. Noah watched from across the creek, a crooked grin on his face.

"It's not like you." Kincaid rode up beside him. "You've been visiting Alex pretty regularly. I guess frequent doses of sex with a gorgeous blonde makes you nicer."

"Shut up, Kincaid." Brett didn't need to be teased himself. "I—"

A rifle shot echoed through the morning, startling everyone including the cattle. Three of the steers took off running and started a stampede. Loud bellows and the power of eight hundred bovine hooves thundered around them. Dust clouds soon choked the air and Brett lost sight of Mason.

"Circle around behind with Noah!" he shouted to Kincaid. "Run them toward the canyon at the edge of the Northwest corner."

Kincaid saluted and took off running after the herd on the east side. Noah was on the west and Brett the south. The panic wouldn't subside however until he found Mason. Soon the sound of a horse screaming reached Brett's ears. He saw the paint floundering in the middle of the herd as they passed him. The horse ran into the stampeding cattle, confused and scared. He'd only been broken a year earlier and hadn't been used much with the herd. Brett regretted his choice of mounts for the boy. It might have cost him his life.

Brett lay low on the horse and raced for the exact spot he'd seen the young paint. The cattle ran all around him with sharp hooves and rolling eyes. He spotted Mason hanging on the side of the saddle, his feet nearly touching the ground with his head dangerously close to the horns speeding past him. Brett leaned to the right to swoop in and grab Mason by the collar and yank him onto his saddle.

A quick flip and the boy sat behind him on the saddle. "Hang on!"

Brett moved through the herd like a fish in a current, slowly but surely heading for the grove of trees to the left. Just as he broke free from the herd, one of the damn steers turned his head and gored Brett's leg. He saw it coming and twisted, avoiding the worse of it. His chaps protected him some, but the horn penetrated deep enough to cause excruciating agony. A shout ripped from his throat as his gorge threatened. Finally he made it to the edge of the grass.

Warm blood bathed his leg. Brett brought the horse to a stop and Mason jumped off, still shaking like a leaf. He gulped air and rubbed his hands on his thighs, then he caught sight of Brett's leg.

"Holy shit."

"Give me your neckerchief." Brett took his and used it as a tourniquet, then took Mason's and wrapped it around the wound. He grunted when he pulled the makeshift bandage taut. "God that hurts."

"Th-thank you, boss. You saved my life."

"No thanks necessary, Mason. A ranch is only as good as the people who work it. You're a good man, kid. I'd hate to lose you."

Mason blinked rapidly. "Ain't nobody ever called me good afore, or a man."

"About time someone did then."

Brett scanned the horizon and saw the cloud of dust the herd kicked up. He couldn't see them anymore, and he needed to get going to help Noah and Kincaid. Particularly since Kincaid had no idea what to do.

"Stay her by the creek, Mason. I'll be back."

"What about your l—"

"I'll take care of it later. It'll do for now. Keep an eye out for the paint, he might head back this way after he breaks free of the herd." With a grimace of pain, Brett kneed his horse into motion and after his cattle.

He caught up to them in twenty minutes, the herd already showing signs of slowing down. Thank God it wasn't a bigger herd, a stampede could last for hours with too many spooked cattle. His leg throbbed in tune with his heart. Fortunately, the blood hadn't leaked through the neckerchief yet. He'd be okay for at least another two or three hours.

He circled around to Noah who looked dirty and weary. "They're getting tired," he shouted.

Brett signaled to start to turn the herd back toward the grazing pasture. He caught Kincaid's eye and waved his hand in the air. Together the three men started pushing the herd around. Good thing the half-Hereford cattle had shorter horns or Brett would be dead from being gored.

By the time they made it back to the pasture, Brett shook from exhaustion and blood loss. No doubt he had to go see Alex, but first he had to find out what happened. Mason held the reins of the paint by the creek with relief written on his young face.

"What happened?" Brett asked Kincaid when the herd finally settled in.

"I heard the report from the rifle. It came from the northwest on that ridge. Damn good shot too, had to be three hundred yards away." The dark-haired man pointed to a rocky outcropping. "I'm guessing it was Ford doing his master's bidding."

"That's my guess too. Lousy son of a bitch."

Kincaid's eyebrows went up when he spotted Brett's bloody bandage. "What the hell happened?"

"Mason's mount got caught up in the stampede. I pulled the boy free, but one of the damn steers caught me."

Kincaid took off his neckerchief and handed it to Brett. "You ought to go see your lady doctor considering you look like shit."

"I'd say shut up, Kincaid, but I don't have the energy. You and Noah keep an eye on the herd for a while. Mason can spot you."

Brett secured the extra neckerchief on his leg while his horse drank his fill from the stream. Fortunately his canteen was full so he didn't need to get off the horse. He had a feeling if he dismounted, he wouldn't get back up again. Pretty soon his wife-to-be would think he was an accident-prone idiot.

CB80

Alex made it back home without incident. She'd half-expected King to stop her from leaving. The wild look in his eye scared her a bit. She'd never been afraid of King before and it bothered her that something had changed. Usually harmless, King had crossed the line into dangerous.

After walking home from the livery, Alex sat for a glass of milk and slice of bread with honey. Her favorite snack always refreshed her. It had been a long, dusty ride, not to mention the tension that had riddled her visit.

She had just sat at the table when she heard the front door open.

"Alex?"

"In the kitchen, Brett." She hoped he was hungry too because she had no desire to skip eating.

"Meet me in the examining room." His gruff command answered that question.

She took a huge bite of the bread with honey and carried her glass with her. She'd have to talk to Brett about ordering her around. That was a condition of marriage. Alex wasn't used to being ordered and found it unpalatable, even from the man she loved.

Chewing quickly, Alex made her way to the examining room. She stopped dead in her tracks when she noticed the trail of blood in the hallway. That blood hadn't been there ten minutes ago, which meant it belonged to Brett.

Alex broke into a run and didn't even remember her feet touching the floor. She found him on the examining table, his right leg covered in blood. He was unbuckling his chaps when she came in. With shaking hands, she set the glass on the counter in the room for fear she'd drop it.

"Hey, Doc, I need a little stitching."

"From the look of it, I'd say a lot of stitching. What happened?" Her heart in her throat, she bit back the impulse to throw herself at him.

"Some bastard stampeded the herd. Got clipped by a steer getting Mason free." He winced as the chaps finally slid free from his right leg.

Alex unbuckled the left side and pulled them off none-too-gently. "How long ago did this happen?"

"Oh, I don't know. I wasn't tracking the time, Alex." He sounded suspiciously like he was fibbing, a very un-Brett-like behavior.

"Uh-huh. I think you're shoveling it faster than I can digest it, Malloy."

Worry for him and his own male stupidity annoyed her to no end. How dare he stay out, putting the well-being of bovine in front of his own health? She went back to the kitchen to retrieve some hot water and hopefully calm herself down.

By the time she walked back to the examining room with a pan of water, she'd convinced herself to focus on treating him, then yell at him later. Brett had managed to shuck his pants and sat only in a pair of drawers and a shirt, a bloody towel pressed to his thigh. Alex's body heated at the sight of her half-naked lover.

"Just trying to save you some time. Don't look at me like I've got two heads."

"I-I'm not. I was just surprised that's all. You're a beautiful man, Brett. I can't help my reaction even if you are bleeding all over." She enjoyed the startled expression that crossed his face.

She washed her hands then gathered the supplies to treat him. After cleaning the wound, she was pleased to note it was only four inches deep at an angle, so the bone wasn't damaged. He hissed instead of breathed while she examined him.

After threading the needle, she looked at him and said, "This is going to hurt. Do you want me to give you laudanum?"

"No, the last time you did I acted like a fool, didn't I?"

"That was the loss of blood, not the laudanum, Brett." With a quick kiss, she went to work suturing him up. Small, neat, even sutures were her specialty. During medical training, she'd practiced constantly on pigs' feet. It paid off in spades.

"Damn, you're good." He'd been watching her, probably to keep his mind off the pain.

"Thanks." She snipped off the remaining catgut. "Let's get a bandage on there."

As Alex wound a clean bandage around his thigh, her hand brushed his testicles. He nearly jumped a country mile.

"Sorry," she mumbled, trying to focus on her task.

"You did that on purpose."

"No, I didn't." Alex cupped him and squeezed. "You'll know when I do."

His gaze locked on hers. "Woman, you spin me in circles."

Alex smiled. "Good. Then I'm doing my job."

He shook his head. "I can tell being married to you won't be boring."

"Never that." With a wink, Alex finished off the bandage then gathered up the bloody clothes. "I'll get you a pair of Papa's trousers to wear. They'll get you home anyway."

Brett grabbed her arm and pulled her toward him. When his lips descended on hers, she held her breath and savored the moment. Soft, yet firm, he demanded entry and she complied. His hot, wet kisses made her toes curl and her pussy throb with arousal.

When he let her mouth loose, she wobbled on her feet a bit.

"Hurry back."

With a nod, she ran from the room, throwing the filthy clothes in the basket in the kitchen, then upstairs to get the trousers. Her father was snoring on his bed when she came in and took a pair of his oldest pants. The smell of whiskey pervaded the air. Sadness for her father started to intrude, but she squelched it. Brett waited downstairs and Alex had to start living her life for herself.

She raced back downstairs in record time, locking the front door before heading back in to Brett. He stood, testing his leg by walking around the room.

"How does it feel?" Alex set the trousers on the examining table and crossed her arms under her breasts. His gaze locked on her chest and the nipples hardened under the scrutiny.

"What?"

"The leg. How does it feel?"

"Sore as hell, but I'll be fine." He limped over to her. "You look pretty today in that blue dress."

"Thank you. I didn't want anyone to see the bruises when I went out."

His entire body stilled. "Went out where?"

Oops. She hadn't meant to let that slip. In for a penny, in for a pound.

"I went to see King to tell him to stop the legal action and leave you alone."

Brett's jaw tightened. "Did you go alone?"

"Will you be angry if I said yes?"

"Dammit, Alex! Someone beat the shit out of you less than two weeks ago and you go gallivanting around the countryside alone? Not only that but to see that pompous ass King who's trying to take my ranch?" He shouted because he loved her, she knew that, but it still hurt.

"I'm a big girl, Brett. I can take care of myself. I had a pistol in my reticule and besides, King would never hurt me." She was absolutely certain of that.

"Oh yeah? So why didn't he look surprised when I told him about your beating?"

Brett's words echoed in her ears. King knew about the beating? He knew? Her mouth opened but nothing came out.

"You have to be more careful, Alex. For my sake. I'll be swinging from the nearest tree for murder if anyone ever touches you again."

Alex knew he meant it too. Although Brett hadn't said "I love you" yet, he had told her so in actions.

"I love you, too."

She wrapped her arms around his neck and kissed him with all that was in her heart. Brett leaned back against the wall and pulled her flush against him. The feel of his firm chest against her hardened nipples was arousing as hell. She rubbed them back and forth, teasing both she and Brett.

"Mm, you feel good."

He chuckled against her lips. "So do you."

His hands roamed down her body, lightly touching, caressing as he went. His staff lengthened and pressed against her belly. A shiver snaked down her spine at the thought of being intimate with Brett again.

"You were injured today," she whispered. "Are you sure you're up to it?"

"Oh, I'm definitely up to it."

Alex bit his bottom lip lightly. "There's that sense of humor again."

"I wasn't being funny. I'm up for anything."

He placed kisses all along her jaw until he reached her ear. His hot breath on her ear sent a throb through her. In all her sexual experiences, she hadn't been as excited as she was now by simple kisses and body contact. Just touching him incited her like wildfire, heated her to the point of conflagration. Her heart beat with a joy it had never known, in perfect tune with her body. It assured her it was much, much more than merely sex.

Brett inched her skirt up until his warm hands made contact with her drawers. She held her breath as fingers dipped into her pussy. A moan burst from her throat at the delicious rasp from his callused skin.

"You like that?"

"God, yes."

He pushed inside her, a slow, leisurely motion simulating the penetration she craved. She rode his hand as the pleasure grew stronger and tingles radiated through her.

"You feel like sweet honey, Alex. I need to taste you."

Before she knew it, he picked her up and set her on the examining table. Her skirt, drawers and blouse were quickly shed and he knelt in front of her with barely a wince. Brett must be caught in the same sexual tornado that enveloped her. She'd never had a man touch her with his mouth and the anticipation made her arousal much stronger.

"Have you ever done this before?" Alex gasped.

"No, but I'm about to."

Brett kissed her thighs as his thumbs parted her nether lips. The first touch of his lips on her hot flesh made her quiver. The second made her groan. By the time his tongue joined in, she could hardly see straight, so she closed her eyes and swam in a sea of amazing pleasure.

"Brett, I..."

"Come for me, you taste so sweet. Come on."

He started finger fucking her and sucking her clit and the stars exploded in, around and through Alex. She cried out his name, gripping the examining table with enough force to pull the sheets out from under her weight.

Alex could barely form a coherent thought. She'd never known such pleasure existed from a man's mouth. He pushed his drawers down and entered her in one swift stroke. The wet slide of his hardness into her pulsing softness nearly drove her over the edge again.

"So tight, God, so tight." He latched onto her breast through the chemise and sucked it.

Alex moaned and wrapped her legs around his hips, pulling him closer. Again and again he thrust into her, almost touching her womb, touching her heart. As his mouth pleasured her breasts, his cock pleasured her pussy.

"Soon, Brett, again," she ground out.

His teeth bit into her nipple and an orgasm ripped through Alex like a tornado. It left her whirling and spinning in a place she'd never been. A vortex of passion that made her gasp for air. Brett shouted her name and thrust into her deeply. As his warm seed joined her body, Alex wept with joy over what she'd rediscovered hiding on a ranch in Cheshire, Wyoming.

Her perfect mate.

Chapter Twelve

Brett made it back home after dark that night. He and Alex spent several hours exploring various nooks and crannies in her house two people could fit in. His body was as wrung dry as his dick. In between the stampede, the thigh wound and the incredible sex, Brett could sleep for days.

As he rode into the Square One, he found Kincaid waiting for him on the porch. Brett dismounted gingerly, then walked his horse over to the barn. Kincaid fell into step beside him.

"That was a long visit to the doc. I was about to send Noah to see if you made it."

"Yeah, I made it. Alex had to stitch it up, but it's not as bad as the shoulder wound. Went in at an angle so it wasn't as deep." Brett wasn't about to tell Kincaid the other reason for taking so long. No doubt he'd tease him anyway.

"Uh-huh. Okay if that's all you're going to say about it. Although I'm curious where you got those britches since they're about four inches too short."

"Shut up, Kincaid."

The ex-gunslinger laughed so hard Brett saw tears squirting from the other man's eyes. He didn't see what was so funny so he kept on walking to the barn. By the time he had Rusty unsaddled and rubbed down, Kincaid had gotten control of his laughing.

174

"Your branding iron arrived today. Some young kid who said he was the smithy's son brought it by. Said he had a girl out at Casey's place so he saved you a trip."

His branding iron. The symbol of the Square One ranch.

"Where is it?"

"Over by the tools. I hung it up on one of the hooks."

Brett limped out of Rusty's stall and headed straight for the tools. The branding iron hung there as the other tools did. He took it down and held it in his hands, closing his eyes to feel the weight of it. Gripping the handle, he trembled.

His brand.

After a few deep breaths, he opened his eyes and examined it. A square with a line down the middle, exactly as he pictured it. Damn it felt good to hold that brand. Not quite as good as holding Alex, but a natural intoxication he could never get from whiskey.

Goddamn, he felt great.

"Doesn't your leg hurt?" Kincaid watched from a few feet away.

"Nah, I've forgotten all about it." Not entirely true, but the throbbing ache wasn't enough to spoil his mood.

"Mason hasn't. In fact, he wouldn't get back on that paint for nothing today. Noah and I had to take split shifts watching the herd."

"What do you mean?" He finally heard what Kincaid said. "He's afraid of the horse or of riding?"

"Both, I think. That stampede scared the shit out of Mason. He's in his room now hiding."

Brett felt bad leaving Kincaid and Noah to watch over his cattle alone, but hell, he'd been wounded. After hanging the brand back up, Brett left the barn and headed for the house to try and stop a bad situation from becoming worse.

Noah must've been out keeping watch on the spooked cattle because the house was empty except for Mason. He could hear the boy moving around in his room. When Brett opened the bedroom door, he found Mason packing his things into a burlap sack.

"Where the hell do you think you're going?"

Mason's eyes were full of confusion and fear. "I ain't no good on a ranch if I'm afraid of the damn cows."

"That's a load of shit. You're not afraid of the cows. Any man would quake in his boots if they went down during a stampede. Hell, I shook for hours afterward. A twelve hundred pound steer ain't nothing to sneeze at." Brett sat on the edge of the bed. "I haven't fired you and I won't."

"I can quit."

"That'd just be stupid. You've got it good here, Mason. Friends, a job, a comfortable bed and food in your belly. Why would you leave?" Brett hoped he didn't leave. They had all grown to love the scruffy kid.

"'Cause I ain't never been good at nothing." Mason sat heavily on the side of the bed. "My ma was right."

"I don't know what your ma told you, but she was wrong. You are good as a cowboy. A natural I'd say. You picked up the lasso in only a week, and you're better than Kincaid with it already. Noah said the same thing to me this morning."

Mason's eyes lit with a tiny bit of hope. "Really?"

"Hell yes. Kincaid can't hit a fence post with a lasso much less a cow." Brett patted Mason's shoulder. "I don't want you to leave and I'm not telling you to leave, but you're a man now. Make your own decision."

Brett stood and looked down at him, wondering if he'd ever been that young and old at the same time. "See you in the morning."

As he left the bedroom, he was pleased to see Mason removing his clothes from the burlap sack. The day from hell had turned into a day Brett would remember for a very long time.

In the morning, all four of the Square One cowboys headed out together to start the branding. A bit late in the season, but nonetheless, Brett knew he had to rebrand his cattle fast or risk rustling. They set up a fire near the outer edge of the pasture, far enough away from the herd that the smoke shouldn't bother them.

It took nearly the whole day and a lot of wrangling from Brett and Noah, but the two hundred cows were officially branded by the time the sun set. Dirty, tired and smiling, they celebrated by going into town for a meal at the restaurant. After washing up, of course.

Noah agreed to stay on the Square One for two months and Brett was more than glad to have his help. It seemed things were turning around for Brett.

Except of course for the legal claim hanging over his head.

CB80CB80

King waited until he saw Alexandra leave the house for the Goodson's store. As soon as she stepped inside the store, King entered the Brighton's house. Byron wasn't downstairs which meant he was probably still sleeping off his drink from the night before.

The ugly mutt was lying in a basket in the examining room and King made sure the door was shut securely. King didn't want to be interrupted by anyone or anything.

Time to get serious with the Brightons, starting with the old man. King wasn't about to allow Alexandra to marry that moron Malloy. She was *his*. Malloy might have fucked her, but King would have her. What King wanted, King got. He'd always wanted Alex to be in his bed and the mother of his children. After marrying two women who bore him nothing but annoyance, he needed a smart, sturdy woman who could give him the heirs he wanted. Alex was that woman.

He had taken his time, buttering her up, then Malloy had to come in and ruin all his plans. Bastard. How could King have a kingdom without a queen?

Sure as the sun rises, King found Byron sound asleep in his bed. He slapped the grizzled cheeks twice before the old man blinked and opened his eyes.

"King?"

"Get up, Byron. We need to talk."

Byron looked almost comical as he wiped his eyes and tried to focus on King.

"What are you doing here? Does Alex know you're upstairs?"

Tired of waiting, King yanked Byron up by his arms and shook him. "We need to talk. Now. Get up and get dressed."

Byron shivered as he slipped off the nightshirt and into his clothes. "I still don't know what you're doing here."

King dragged Byron from his room and down the hall. "You need to talk some sense into your daughter. She says she's going to marry Malloy, but that ain't gonna happen. You are going to force her to marry me."

Byron tugged on his arm. "I will do no such thing. Brett is a good man and exactly what Alex needs."

"No." King leaned down and shouted into Byron's face. "*I'm* exactly what she needs."

"No, you're not." Byron stopped four feet from the stairs and put his hands on his hips. "You cannot make me do anything, King."

"Oh yes I can." King pulled Byron by the arms, dragging him down the carpet runner as easily as a child.

"Let go of me this instant, King Dawson! I will report you to Sheriff Weissman for this."

King whipped Byron around and started pushing at his shoulders. How dare he threaten a Dawson with the law? A Dawson made his own law.

"Who do you think you are? You can't defy me, old man. I will make your life a living hell." He pushed again and Byron's arms swung around madly as he tried to regain his balance. "That little demonstration on Alex? That was just a small taste of what I can do."

Byron grabbed King by the throat in a surprisingly strong grip. "You? You did that to her?"

King didn't take too kindly to anyone touching him without permission. He brought his fist back and punched Byron in the chest. The old doctor sailed through the air almost halfway down the stairs before landing with a loud crack on the wooden steps below.

After a few moments, the damn dog started barking. With a frown, King stomped down the steps, annoyed the old man had fought him. He stepped over the body and walked to the door.

No need trying to convince Byron any longer, it was much too late for that. King left and headed for the saloon.

CB8O8O

Alex leisurely walked home with her basket on her arm. Although some gray clouds threatened, it hadn't rained yet and she was enjoying the fresh air. Enjoying being alive and in love.

Brett promised to come by every chance he could and Alex knew he'd be by that evening since he hadn't the night before. God knows she was worn out from their afternoon romping. He'd be twice as worn out since he'd been injured during the day. Her cheeks heated with the remembrance of how she'd seduced Brett after doctoring his wound. Every day was a gift and she wasn't about to let one slip through her fingers.

Alex had purchased some special fixings for a supper of beef stew and dumplings. Goodson's also had a supply of fresh eggs Alex snatched up for the noon meal with her father. He loved eggs and bacon, and without any laying hens it was a delicacy he savored when he could.

She heard Ug barking as soon as she walked up to the front door. That was a good sign. He hadn't barked much since his injuries and the sound was like music to her ears. Alex stepped inside and headed for the examining room.

"Ug, I'm so glad to hear you bark." She opened the door and he ran from the room heading straight for the stairs.

Dread coated her body and made her shiver with fear. She forced herself to walk toward the stairs, knowing whatever she found would not be good. Ug was frantic now, barking and whining. Alex rounded the corner and the basket landed on the floor in front of her.

Her father lay at the bottom of the stairs, his head at an impossible angle, his mouth open in an eternal scream. His pipe he always kept in his pocket lay broken beside him. Blood oozed from his mouth and his eyes appeared to beseech her for help. Alex didn't remember dropping to her knees, but she found herself kneeling in broken egg shells and sobbing.

Oh, God, Papa.

Alex checked her father to be certain he was truly dead, crying until her stomach hurt. After confirming it, she took a sheet from the nearby linen closet and covered him. Ug sat next to the body, guarding him, it seemed, even after death.

"I'm going to get the sheriff, Ug. You take care of him, okay, boy?"

Ug woofed and his eyes almost appeared to offer her sympathy. She kissed his furry head and stood. Alex walked back out the door a different person.

ෞ෫ඓ෭

Brett rode into Cheshire later than he intended. It had been two days since he'd left Alex's arms and he missed her, a bittersweet feeling he didn't want to get used to. As soon as he could, he'd make Alex his wife, then he wouldn't have to ride an hour just to see her.

When he turned down Alex's street, every light in the Brighton house was on. Looked like a Christmas tree. Something was wrong.

Brett broke into a gallop and arrived in seconds flat. Knowing Rusty would stay put, he jumped down and ran into the house as fast as his sore leg would let him.

"Alex?"

"In here."

He followed the sound of her voice to the parlor. She sat on the settee with Ug at her feet. The look in her eyes nearly unmanned him—haunted, devastated and heartbroken.

He sat beside her, wrapping his arm around her shoulders.

"What happened?"

"Papa," she whispered brokenly. "He's d-dead."

Dead? Byron was dead? He was still angry at the old man's meddling, but he surely didn't wish him harm.

Brett pulled her onto his lap and held her close, stroking and soothing her. She cried quietly against his shirt, never screaming or ranting. Alex was every inch the lady, even when drowning in grief.

Jim appeared in the doorway and caught Brett's eye.

Brett gestured with his hand to Jim. "You might as well come in and tell both of us. Alex would never forgive me if you didn't."

She wiped her eyes with a handkerchief and glanced up at the sheriff as he sat on the other end of the settee. The dark-haired lawman took off his hat and fiddled with it.

"It appears your father had help down those stairs."

"What does that mean?" Brett snapped.

"It means there's signs of a struggle upstairs. The carpet runner is all cockeyed, and I found some dirt on the floor in Byron's room and the hallway. The same dirt in the foyer and nobody's shoes in this house are muddy." Jim glanced apologetically at Alex. "I'm sorry, Doc. I wish to hell it had been an accident."

"So do I." She took a deep breath and let it out in a gust. "Is there any sign of who did it?"

Jim shook his head. "Nothing specific. Byron wasn't a big man. It wouldn't take much to overpower him. Do you know of anyone who might want to hurt him?"

Alex and Brett glanced at each other, the same name on their lips.

"King Dawson."

"King? Why would he want to hurt Byron?"

Brett waited until Alex nodded before he spoke. "I asked Alex to marry me and King didn't take too kindly to the idea. Aside from that, he's got some legal action against me with a man claiming to be old Martin's son."

Jim's eyebrows jumped. "You two are getting hitched? I'm glad to hear that." He shook Brett's hand. "I thought you two ought—"

"Jim, about King."

"Yeah, right. Sorry. So he was angry about the wedding and he's trying to get you off your ranch?"

"That about sums it up. Aside from that, I think he was behind the attack on Alex, too." Just remembering that she'd been hurt made Brett's fists clench. How much could one family endure?

"Unfortunately without evidence or a witness, there isn't anything I can do about your theories, Brett." Jim stood and put his hat on his head. "Alfred's already taken your father down to get him ready for burial. I'll tell folks to come by the cemetery around nine in the morning. Is that okay with you, Doc?"

"Yes, th-that's fine." She huddled closer to Brett.

"In the meantime, I'll start looking into King's whereabouts this morning." Jim inclined his head at Alex. "Brett, I'll see you later."

Brett understood that to mean he'd give more details when Alex wasn't around. Regardless of what she may want to know, she was in no shape to handle any more harsh news.

After Jim left, Brett continued to hold Alex, glad he could be there for her and wishing he'd arrived earlier.

"How's your leg? I'm not hurting you, am I?"

"Oh, honey, don't worry about my leg. You couldn't possibly hurt me sitting on my lap." He breathed in her scent, glad Alex hadn't been home when Byron was killed. God knows what would have happened to her then.

"You need to come back to the Square One with me." After saying it out loud, he knew it was the right thing to do. He couldn't protect her if he was an hour away, and he couldn't leave his ranch for fear of what King would do next. They needed to huddle together.

"No, I can't. There are patients who need my help."

"Alex, we can send them out to the ranch if they need help. I can't keep an eye on you all the way from home. And I think I'll lose my mind if I can't protect you." He had to make her see reason. "Please, honey."

"I don't think I've ever heard you say please." She lifted her head and turned her watery gaze on him. "It must be serious then."

"Yes, it is." He cupped her cheek. "We'll bring Rowdy and rent a buggy to carry your things. I...I'll go plumb loco if you stay here by yourself." He didn't want to resort to begging, but if necessary, he'd do it.

"I don't want the murderer to think he ran me out of my own house." Her words protested, but her expression said something different.

"We'll kick Kincaid out of the bedroom and put a chair under the knob for you."

She looked surprised. "You would stay with me?"

"Always."

Alex searched his eyes looking for whatever she needed to find. "I'll come, but only for a few days."

Brett breathed a huge sigh of relief inside. "Thank you. I know it's not easy for you to retreat."

"About as easy as it is for you. Now help me pack, cowboy. I'll need to bring a medical bag with supplies as well as some books to pass the time."

He helped her to her feet then stood and gathered her close for a hug. The full impact of Byron's murder hit him and he shook at the implications of it. Alex wouldn't be safe until she was his wife and the Square One was his free and clear.

It seemed as though a warning was in order. He was sure Kincaid would be happy to help Brett deliver it.

CBRROBO

Without much ado, Alex and Ug moved into the Square One. The four male residents treated her like a queen and she didn't have to do chores for herself. They fetched water, wood, food and anything else she wanted. They even washed and dressed to escort her to her father's funeral. Alex felt proud to have Brett on her arm and three solid male presences behind her.

Perhaps Brett had been right to say she needed protection. Their fussing was comforting and made her feel safe. Her heart ached with the loss of her father. The mood on the ride into town grew more somber as each mile passed. Alex had put three handkerchiefs in her reticule, knowing she would likely use every one of them.

When the cemetery came into view, a small sob escaped Alex at the sight of the lonely burial ground. She wanted to scream at God for taking her papa too soon. He had so many years left and seemed to be finally giving up drinking. It wasn't fair.

Of course, all of Alex's protests were selfish. She missed him terribly and so many times over the last day she'd wanted to talk to him. A particular passage in a book or something she needed to tell him would pop into her head and then she'd remember he was gone. Gone for the rest of her life.

As she stepped from the buggy, Alex straightened her shoulders and went to do the hardest task for the second time in her life.

The entire town turned out for Byron's funeral, stories were told and tears shed. Alex stared at the pine coffin as they lowered it into the ground. As she tossed a handful of dirt over her father's remains, she made a silent vow to bring his killer to justice.

"I love you, Papa. I hope you're in Mama's arms right now looking down on me. I miss you both so much."

Her voice broke and Alex struggled to maintain control. Just as she thought her trembling would overcome her, Brett appeared at her elbow to steady her.

"Come on, honey. Let's go sit down and let other folks pay their respects."

Alex leaned on Brett and allowed him to lead her to the shade of an oak tree. There he rested against the tree and tucked her under his arm. She closed her eyes and spent the rest of the funeral remembering how much she loved her father and how much she'd miss him.

Chapter Thirteen

The day after the funeral Brett and Kincaid set out before breakfast and headed northeast to the Dawson ranch. Each wore pistols and had a rifle secured to the saddle. Brett wanted to make sure they were well armed to survive an ambush or anything else King decided to lob at them.

The battle lines had been drawn. Brett just needed to accept the challenge King had thrown in his face. No more sitting on his ranch and waiting for something to happen because something *had* happened. Byron had been murdered and Alex beaten.

No more.

The litany ran through Brett's head as they galloped across the land rich with green and life. It was a wonder more men didn't kill for it. As they approached the main gate, Kincaid hissed.

"I see at least six armed men. One of them is Ford. I'd recognize that scarecrow of death anywhere."

"What do you think we should do?" Brett was a rancher, not a gunfighter. He'd had his share of rescue operations with his family, but nothing this personal. Nothing that put his future at stake.

"Slow to a trot and let's ease up there. They can't just gun us down if we're being neighborly." Kincaid's grin was anything but neighborly.

They slowed the horses and trotted the last quarter mile to the gate. All six men stood with rifles pointed toward the sky, but the feeling of menace flowed strongly from each one.

Ford strolled toward them, his cold expression dropping the August temperature by ten degrees. "Something I can help you boys with?"

Kincaid snorted. "You're twenty-five years old, Ford. Who are you calling a boy?"

"Don't rile him," Brett whispered harshly. "I need you alive."

"Couldn't help it. He makes my hackles jump." Kincaid's lips barely moved.

"Me, too."

Ford's eyes narrowed. "What do you want?"

"We want to talk to King." Brett kept his voice steady and sure. He didn't want any of those fools knowing his heart was about to burst from his chest and his hands were as clammy as a whore in church.

"He don't want to talk to you. Now git before I shoot you for trespassing." Ford's grin made the horses whinny.

"How about you give him a message from me?"

Ford cocked one black eyebrow. "What would that message be?"

"Tell him I know what he did to Byron and Alex Brighton. I demand he drop the legal battle and never speak to Alex again. Tell him if he doesn't, the Malloys are declaring war." It felt good to say it. Damn good. Liberating even.

"You sure you want me to deliver that?" Ford's hand drifted toward the pistol riding low on his thigh.

"More than sure. I can deliver it myself if you'd like." Rusty danced nervously beneath him and Brett calmed the gelding with his knees.

"I'll deliver the message. You and your dog just better be sure you're ready for the battle. I never knew a piece of pussy was worth your life."

Brett nearly flew off the horse to punch the piece of shit, but Kincaid's arm on his chest stopped him.

"I'll bet you haven't," Kincaid drawled. "My guess is you've never even had real pussy before."

Someone snickered beside Ford. He snapped his head toward the offending guard and shot the man dead in the time it took to blink. Brett knew then Kincaid wasn't kidding about Ford being dangerous. He wasn't just dangerous, he was as crazy as King.

"Get the fuck off Dawson land." Ford seemed to vibrate with fury. His colorless eyes sparked beneath the rim of his black hat.

"Just deliver the message."

Brett and Kincaid wheeled their horses around and broke out into a full gallop. They both leaned low in the saddle waiting for the report of a rifle as they raced back toward the Square One.

Brett wasn't sure throwing down the gauntlet to two crazy men had been the best idea in the world, but it felt good. He was tired of doing nothing. Time to visit Ray and make a plan for action.

The Malloys were being called to war.

CRKOBO

Alex had been on the Square One ranch for three days and she felt trapped. There weren't any women to talk to, nowhere to visit, and during the day, not a soul around but herself. Brett did his best to make her comfortable, but it didn't feel like enough. She needed him near her always.

It wasn't as if she didn't love Brett, because she did. Sleeping alone wasn't exactly what she had in mind, but he refused to compromise her reputation with the other men on the ranch. It was sweet, but unsatisfying. She'd been more intimate with him when they lived an hour apart.

She wiped the last plate dry as she stared out the small window by the sink. Brett and Kincaid had rushed to install a new sink so she didn't have to go to the well pump for water. They were all gentlemen and she appreciated their kindness more than they knew.

Mason stayed behind to "help" her at the ranch, but Alex knew the real reason he stayed was to keep them both safe. He was a good kid and a good worker. He was out mucking the stalls in the barn while she did the dishes.

With a sigh, she set the tin plate on top of the others on the shelf and hung the towel on the side of the sink to dry. Ug had found a cat in the barn to make friends with and now spent a good portion of his time visiting with his kitty. They were like kindred spirits, both stray animals that found homes and each other. The little tabby had taken to Ug, although she acted a bit superior to the floppy-eared dog.

Alex was unused to being alone and had finished all the books she'd brought. She didn't like needlepoint or anything along those lines. That left writing, which she'd done enough of to make a dent in her middle finger from the pencil. Truth was,

Alex was bored and had too much time on her hands to think. Her father had been on her mind quite a bit, as had Brett and the untenable legal situation.

The temperature hovered on the far side of hot, but Alex needed to get out of the house before she started climbing the walls. She grabbed her sun bonnet and headed outside into the sticky air. Not the most pleasant weather, typical for late summer, but anything was better than staring at the cabin walls.

Alex walked toward the corral to visit Rowdy. The gelding had started to get fat since he hadn't been ridden much in the last three weeks. He whickered and trotted right over to her.

"You miss me, boy? Me, too. I need to go for a ride."

Rowdy nudged her hand and butted his head against her shoulder.

"I'll take that as a yes. Let me see if my guard wants to come."

She walked into the barn and found Mason returning from emptying the wheelbarrow into the pile behind the barn.

"All done?"

"Yes'm. Is there somethin' you wanted me to do?" He wiped his forehead with one dirty arm leaving a smear across his skin.

Alex pretended not to notice.

"I wanted to go for a ride since it's such a beautiful day. Would you like to go with me? I'll pack a picnic lunch and we can sit by the creek and watch the rest of the cowboys work."

He looked hesitant, perhaps even a little scared. Brett had told her the stampede had frightened him quite a bit.

"I haven't ridden my horse in weeks. He's getting fat and lazy, so I'll only be able to trot. If you won't be too bored, I'd really love the company."

Mason glanced at the paint in the stall beside him and shuffled his feet back and forth. "I dunno."

"I'll even bring a book and I can read to you."

"Really, for true?" His face lit as if from a light within.

"Yes, of course." She wanted to give his skinny body a hug, but knew he'd take it as a sign of weakness. Even if he was the same height as she, he was still a boy and succumbed to the whole "I need to be a man" edict.

"Okay, then, I'll saddle the horses while you get the food."

"Excellent!" Alex headed back into the house to hunt up something to carry their lunch in. She'd bring extra so Brett, Noah and Kincaid could share. Within ten minutes they were on their way with a lunch of canned peaches, biscuits and honey, lemonade, and cold chicken packed in Ug's basket. Alex had wiped out the inside and wrapped the food in a sheet they could also use to sit on for their picnic.

On the ride out to the pasture, she chatted with Mason and tried to keep him at ease on the horse. Before she knew it, they'd arrived at the creek and dismounted. Alex sat on the bank and read some of *Robinson Crusoe* to Mason. He watched her finger move beneath the words as she wove the tale with her voice.

Soon he wanted to learn some of the letters, and picked up common words quickly. By the time she was ready to eat, several hours had passed and the rest of the men rode up. Mason seemed embarrassed to be reading, but Brett put him at ease.

"Reading is important to any man, Mason. You need to make sure no one ever cheats you at anything. If you can't read, they will. Besides, ladies love a man who reads poetry to them."

Alex chuckled under her breath. Brett had never read a word of poetry, much less to her. They all sat on the sheet and ate the delicious lunch together. The camaraderie flowed strongly between them, like a small family.

All too soon, the food was gone and it was time to return. Brett must have seen something in her face because he told the others he had to go back to the ranch. Alex's heart skipped a beat at the thought they might be going back together for an afternoon dessert.

All three galloped back to the ranch, laughing and racing each other. By the time they arrived, Alex was out of breath and smiling like a lunatic. Even Brett smiled and her body reacted like a match to flame.

"Here, Mason, why don't you take this book and practice?"

"Really?" He held the book like a precious gift. "I can have it?"

"You can have it for as long as you like." Alex's gaze focused on Brett's lips and what she'd like to do with them in the next minute.

"Thanks!" Mason led the horses into the barn, book tucked into his pocket.

"Now that he's gone..." Alex wrapped her arm around Brett's. "I have something to show you in the house."

"Can't wait," he murmured.

He opened the door for her and she stepped into a nightmare. Gone was the clean, tidy house she'd left four hours earlier. In its place was a disaster. The smell of horse manure hit her first, then urine. Brett pushed past her and the expression on his face made her heart hurt.

"Holy God."

Every piece of furniture had been smashed into pieces no bigger than kindling. They'd chopped up the shelves and scattered all the food and supplies around the kitchen, then apparently used the sink as a privy. The cookstove had huge dents in the side and the stovepipe was missing with ashes scattered around the room.

The windows all had been cracked or broken. The stones in the fireplace were even hammered so the mortar was coming loose. Brett leaned down and picked up the shattered remnants of the wooden sign Jack had made. His knuckles turned white and she heard the wood creak. After Brett digested the sight of the wreckage he ran towards the bedroom, Alex hot on his heels.

They'd written *whore* in manure on the walls, urinated on the mattress and chopped up the bed. All their clothes were in shreds and scattered on the floor. The second bedroom was in no better shape than the first.

Everything was destroyed. Completely destroyed. Brett's face turned to stone in front of her. She wrapped her arms around him and it felt like embracing a tree.

"I'm so sorry, Brett," she whispered against his shoulder.

"Fucking bastard."

Alex didn't say a word about his language. If she'd been pushed, she might have said something just as bad. Brett had been so proud of the house and in one act of violence, they'd shattered a piece of his heart.

"We'll get started cleaning it up."

He extracted himself from her arms and walked outside. She let him go, understanding he needed some private time to grieve over what they'd taken from him. She glared at the disgusting mess and silently cursed King Dawson for being such an animal. Then she headed for the barn to get Mason.

Brett shook with anger. He had everything he could do not to scream at the top of his lungs in frustration. That bastard King had nothing better to do than destroy things. If he couldn't have it then he broke it, just like a spoiled child.

Alex had retrieved Mason and they started cleaning up the house. He could hear them throwing things into the wheelbarrow, more than likely the furniture Jack had made. Knowing Alex, she'd probably clean the shit and piss next. Being a doctor, cleanliness was of the utmost importance in her world.

Brett stomped over to the well and started pumping the handle. What he really wanted to do was ride over to King's ranch and use his fists instead. Son of a bitch, what a fucking mess.

He brought a bucket of water in and grabbed the other tin bucket to pour it into. The stovepipe was missing so they'd have to start a fire outside to even heat water. He glanced at the wheelbarrow full of furniture pieces. Might as well get some use out of it.

He built up enough stones to contain a fire, then added the pieces of wood. The fire was upwind from the house and far enough away to not be a danger. After the blaze was going, he shifted everything to put the pail on to heat.

Alex kept looking out at him but didn't speak or force him into conversation. She must have sensed he needed some time to himself to calm down. That's something love gave them— understanding. After the first pail of water was hot, he brought it into the house and poured it into the wooden pail.

He sent Mason out to tell Noah and Kincaid what was going on. Brett stood staring out over the land, wondering how to get out of the shit situation he'd gotten in with King. Brett didn't ask for it, but he damn sure would finish it.

Alex touched his shoulder. "Are you okay?"

He turned and gathered her in his arms. "I'm sorry they destroyed your clothes."

She snorted. "My clothes are the least of my worries. They nearly destroyed your house. It will take a week to get it livable."

"At least."

"I didn't finish." She hugged him tightly. "This was a personal attack on both of us and it's because of me. It's all because of me. The stampede, the house, all of it. King wants me and he doesn't care who he hurts to get me." She took a deep breath and blew it out shakily. "I'm sorry."

"Oh, honey." He kissed her temple. "You didn't do anything to be sorry for. That lousy excuse for a human being is trying to force us to do his bidding. The house isn't a reason for you to give in."

"I won't."

Her voice rang true and strong. Brett thanked God again for giving him a woman like Alex to love and be loved by in return. The sound of hoofbeats signaled Mason's return. He stepped back and looked into her eyes. The words "I love you" danced on his tongue, but he couldn't get them out.

"I know," she said with understanding in her eyes. "I love you, too."

With a quick kiss, he let her go and turned back to the fire. Looked like his plan to protect Alex didn't work out too well. King had invaded his home.

After Kincaid had come back for the night, Brett asked him to take a walk. They walked about five minutes from the house before Brett could speak. Kincaid stood and put his hands on his hips, watching Brett as he paced. Ug sat beside him, whining softly.

"You can't protect her every minute."

"Yes, I can. I can. I just failed, again. How the hell can I expect her to marry me when some bastard keeps hurting her and I don't stop it?" Brett's voice broke on the last word as a fresh wave of anger hit him.

Kincaid stopped him with a touch on his shoulder. "Take a breath there. You're making me dizzy with all that pacing."

Brett threw Kincaid's hand off. "I don't really give a shit if you're dizzy. I need to figure out how to stop this before Alex gets hurt again."

Kincaid rubbed his chin with his hand. "You might want to have more than just the two of us before you go hunting that big bastard."

He made a good point. King had dozens of men at his disposal, as evidenced by the half-dozen who stood guard at the gate alone. They needed stealth and smarts, two things Brett could not lay claim to at the moment.

"In the morning, let's go over to Ray's house and make a plan."

Kincaid nodded and headed back toward the house. Ug licked Brett's hand, apparently giving his approval, too. Brett hoped like hell he was right, because if his stupidity cost Alex her life, he'd never forgive himself.

CRE080

"I see you're still living in this shit hole, darlin'."

King's booming voice almost startled her clean out of her wits. Alex had been scrubbing the manure off the walls in the kitchen. She should have known he would show up sooner or later.

She didn't even look at him or her tone wouldn't be calm. "You did enough damage yesterday. Are you happy to force me to live in a barn? Get off this ranch, King."

"I can't do that. You see, you were supposed to marry me. Instead, you chose to get yourself hitched to that idiot Malloy. Not a wise choice, Alexandra."

His hand landed on her shoulder and she immediately stepped out of his grasp and kicked him in the shin. When he yelped in pain, she inwardly grinned.

"Now that wasn't a very nice thing to do to your intended bridegroom."

He sounded annoyed. Good.

"Neither is a beating or destroying someone's property. Those were my clothes you ripped to shreds," she snapped. "How about you leave now and I won't tell the sheriff about it."

He laughed long and hard, the guffaws echoing off the bare chamber walls. "You think I'm going to leave and say sorry? I don't think so. I warned you that you were mine. *Mine*, you bitch. You already spread your legs for that idiot. You're lucky I'll still allow you to be my wife."

Alex was astounded by his brazen twist on truth and reality. "You honestly believe I'll marry you? After all this?"

"Of course you will. You're a smart woman, Alexandra. You see, you leave this room as my wife, or you don't leave it alive. I gave your father that choice and he chose wrongly."

Oh, Papa.

He smacked her on the buttocks so hard, it brought tears to her eyes. She tried to digest his words, but her heart refused to cooperate with the fact King had confessed to murdering her father. Her throat closed with a sob that resonated with agony.

Not only had he killed her father, but either she married him or he'd kill her. It seemed as though she'd fallen into one of the novels she'd read. One where the main villain was insane and evil. King had showed the darkest side of himself, one that made Alex shudder in disgust. She'd never quite liked King, but she'd never been afraid of him until now.

Alex closed her eyes and pictured Brett as he kissed her goodbye that morning.

She'd whispered "I love you" in his ear. Instead of responding in kind, he kissed her neck and squeezed her tight. She could still smell his scent if she concentrated.

"You understand me, woman?" King's voice sliced through her thoughts.

As she stared into his cold, ice blue eyes, the sound of a gun cocking behind her made her smile.

"Mister, I don't know who you are but if you touch Doc Brighton one more time I'm gonna shoot off your pecker. Turn around and leave." Mason almost sounded like a man.

"You heard him, get out."

King's eyes blazed with fire and retribution, making her hackles rise, but she stood firm. He turned around and walked out of the house. Alex grabbed the repeating rifle from Mason.

"Get the other one from behind the bedroom door."

He ran off and was back in seconds, rifle in hand. She nodded and they walked outside together. This time King had brought one man, that creepy one called Ford. They stood outside, talking quietly.

Alex would do everything in her power to fight King and avoid being his wife, even if it meant her own death. The worst thing anyone could do was to give in to a bully.

She would fight with every ounce of her strength. King had no idea what he was up against.

ଓଃ୬ଃ୪ଠ

Brett lassoed the cow and pulled her from the creek with Rusty's help. Dumb thing had wandered in there then couldn't get back up the embankment. At least it wasn't mud. He shuddered at the memory of pulling cattle from the mud—like molasses and taffy with a thousand-pound bovine in the middle.

As he dismounted, Brett thought he imagined Ug barking, but then it got louder. The cattle lowed and scattered a bit as the mutt came running across the pasture like his tail was on fire. Brett's heart began to pound. Ug wouldn't be away from the house unless something was wrong. He never left Alex except to play with the barn cat.

Brett quickly pulled the lasso off the cow and sent her back with the others. Then he jumped up on Rusty and headed toward the dog. They met halfway with Kincaid close on Brett's heels.

"What is it, boy?"

Ug barked and ran around in a circle.

"Wasn't this the dog that was almost dead three weeks ago?" Kincaid sounded impressed.

"He had good doctors." Brett watched in amazement as Ug ran ten yards away then stopped and looked back.

Woof. Woof. Woof.

Sure as hell sounded like "Come on you idiot!" to Brett. He wasn't one to ignore his instincts and they were ringing loud.

"I'm heading back to the house. Something's wrong. Ug wouldn't be out here if it wasn't." Brett started toward the dog and the mutt took off running, looking back to make sure Brett followed.

Kincaid rode up beside him. "You think the dog is that smart?"

"No, I know he's that smart. He saved Alex's life once already." Brett had plenty of dogs in his life, but none of them compared to the scraggly mutt called Ug. He deserved a lifetime of the best food and all the bitches he wanted.

The two men rode in silence, following the dog all the way back to the ranch. He found Alex and Mason both armed, facing down King.

"You have two seconds, King," she said with enough gumption for three women. "Get moving."

"You think a woman and a boy are going to make me do anything?"

The shot startled everyone but Alex. King's hat lay twenty feet away, with a huge damn hole in it. Brett couldn't stop the grin that spread across his face. Damn, he never knew she had it in her.

"Get going."

King looked as if he wanted to say something but instead he mounted his palomino and rode off, Ford at his heels.

Chapter Fourteen

Until the house could be cleaned thoroughly, every patient and visitor had to be greeted in the barn. Not exactly the ideal conditions for a doctor, but Alex didn't complain. She knew it wouldn't help matters. They were all on edge. For more reasons than one.

Brett's parents came by with extra blankets and food, and he accepted the help with a bit more ease than usual. Alex was proud of him for not gunning King down for what he'd done. He even had to convince Ray to let the law and the court handle King's punishment.

The sheriff examined everything and talked to Alex and Mason about what King said. Jim indicated it wouldn't be enough to arrest him, but with some stronger evidence they could. Frustrated and angry, Brett, Noah and Kincaid spent twenty-four hours a day watching the herd. Waiting for the next attack.

Matt Jamison, the attorney from Hawk's Bend, came two days later. A thin, nervous-looking man with red hair and pale skin, he seemed completely intimidated by Brett's quiet intensity.

Alex sat between them on barrels in the barn. "Someone broke in two days ago," she explained to the stranger. "We think it was King Dawson, the same man trying to force Brett off the Square One."

"I, uh, know who Mr. Dawson is." He scratched at his starched collar and glanced at the papers Brett had given him. "I'm not sure there's anything we can do to help you keep the ranch, Mr. Malloy."

Brett's brows drew together in a fierce frown. "What the hell does that mean?"

Matt shuffled the papers in his hand. "If Mr. Samson is the legal heir to the ranch, then you don't have a case."

"Is there evidence that Mr. Samson is the legal heir?" Alex held Brett's hand tightly. She didn't know if it was for his sake or hers.

"I'm sure there is."

Alex started to get the idea Matt was lying to them. Blatantly lying. Perhaps King or one of his henchmen had paid a visit to the young attorney and threatened him. She glanced at Brett and realized he'd come to the same conclusion.

"I'm not going to get angry at you. You need to protect yourself the same as everyone, but I am going to tell you to leave. Now." Brett kept his voice steady and even, but beneath the politeness lay a sharpness he couldn't hide.

Matt dropped the papers, he startled so bad. "I'm not sure what you mean."

"Oh, yes you do." Alex stood and put her hands on her hips. "Mr. Malloy asked you to leave. You can do him the courtesy of complying."

Matt looked between them, his mouth open but no words coming out.

"King Dawson is a bully, Mr. Jamison. He bullies everyone and everything. You are just his latest victim." She walked toward the barn door and slid it open. "Thank you for your time."

With an apologetic look, the young man left the barn and she shut the door behind him.

CRONSO

Francesca and Lily came to help clean the house. Brett was amazed by what three determined women could do together. After two days, the house didn't smell like shit and piss anymore, but it lay empty.

Brett had to order windows again, this time on credit, a situation that made him cringe. When he left Goodson's store, he felt things couldn't get much worse. He was wrong.

"Brett, wait just a minute," Harvey Brown called. He'd been taking care of the mail and telegrams for as long as Brett could remember. Harvey was blessed with snow white hair, a stooped back and sharp brown eyes with a ready smile.

"I've got a letter for you, special delivery. Came from the county seat, it did. I thought I'd send someone out to give it to you but seeing how you're here, it'd save a trip." He handed Brett the thick vellum envelope. "Looks mighty important."

Brett stared at the envelope, thanked Harvey and wandered back to his horse, his gaze riveted on the impending news in his hand. The surprising taste of fear coated his tongue. The return address was the county courthouse.

"Heavy reading there, little brother?" Ray stepped up beside him.

"I think it's about the ranch." He continued to look at the envelope without even glancing at Ray.

"Aren't you going to open it?"

Brett finally looked at Ray. He was holding a couple of tools he must have had the smithy make for him. In his eyes, Brett saw a reflection of his own concern over the contents of the envelope.

"I can't."

After dropping the iron tools on the ground, Ray held out his hand and Brett slowly put the envelope in it. With a quick twist, Ray pulled off the end of the envelope and had the paper unfolded. His eyes moved quickly over the words. Brett was about to burst with curiosity.

"What does it say, dammit?"

Ray folded the paper and put it back in the envelope. "You've got two days until the case is heard by Judge Harris right here in Cheshire."

Two days?

"I...I don't even have a lawyer, Ray. What the hell am I gonna do?" He couldn't seem to get his breathing under control. Brett couldn't lose the ranch, he just couldn't.

Ray took Brett by the shoulders, the envelope crinkling in his hand. "Take a breath and calm down."

Brett focused on his brother's face instead of the sheer panic that threatened. His stomach had taken residence near his heart, and squeezed his lungs so tightly he could hardly get a breath in.

"Listen to me, brother. We'll get a lawyer for you, a good one. King just can't take a ranch when he feels like it, especially one that belongs to a Malloy. Do you hear me?"

"I hear you. I need help, Ray." For the first time in his life, Brett had no qualms about asking for or receiving help. This wasn't about pride or charity, it was about family and love. That's all that mattered in life.

Ray looked at Harvey, who hovered near the door to his little storefront. "Trevor has a friend in Cheyenne who helped Adelaide keep her saloon. Do you remember him?"

Brett remembered him well. "Carson Foster. Kind of an odd man, but smart as hell."

"That's the one. We need to wire Trevor and ask them both to come. Are you ready to do that?" Ray knew Brett and Trevor hadn't spoken in nearly two months.

The situation called for pride to be swallowed and lines to be crossed. Brett might not have done it a month ago. Hell, he might not have done it two weeks ago, but today was a different day. He had a woman he wanted to marry and a ranch he desperately wanted to keep.

"Yes, I'm ready." He glanced at his feet and took a deep breath. "Thank you."

"No need to thank me, little brother. Let's get that telegram sent and see if we can't beat King at his own game." Ray clapped him on the shoulder.

Brett nodded, eager to do something other than run around like a chicken with his head cut off. Ray always helped ground him even when he didn't need it. A solid presence Brett was grateful for.

After Ray picked up his tools, he and Brett walked toward Harvey, ignoring the old man's denials that he didn't hear anything they were talking about. However, he went straight to the telegraph machine and waited like an eager boy on Christmas.

The reply came within an hour. It simply read, "We'll be there tomorrow morning." Brett's telegram had been a bit vague, but he'd asked for help. It appeared Trevor was more than willing to give it. Now Brett had to figure out what to do when Trevor arrived.

ଔୠଓ୭

King drummed his fingers on his desk, staring out into the bright morning sunshine. Nothing had worked. Brett still squatted on the damn ranch and Alexandra refused to marry King. The situation was not to King's liking. Definitely not.

Ford stood beside the desk, polishing one of his pistols. He'd proven to be as ruthless as his reputation, and he took orders well. So far, King had not asked him to kill anyone, but that was about to change.

"Malloy seems to be unmovable and we need to make him move. He's fucking my woman. Probably gave her some kind of disease too so I won't be able to get between her thighs without my dick falling off," he groused. "What about the gunslinger?"

Ford looked up. "Kincaid. I know him."

"Is he good?"

"He's good, but not as good as me."

King pursed his lips and did his best to control the anger threatening to explode. "Get rid of him."

Ford put his gun back in its holster. "Understood. Do you want folks to know it was me or you want it in the dark?"

"Kill him out on the street. Make sure he doesn't get up again. I want Malloy to lose his gun, then I can kill him and get my woman and the land. As soon as you find him, send word." King's eyes narrowed. "Don't fuck this up, Ford, or I'll kill you myself."

One pale eyebrow rose, but the gunslinger didn't respond. Instead, he turned and left the room. King couldn't wait to ride into town for the show.

 C3EOR

Trevor and Carson arrived shortly after breakfast the next morning. Brett was standing outside drinking coffee when he saw them. The morning sun rose behind them, so he was unsure if the visitors were friend or foe until he saw the horse. No mistaking Trevor's horse Silver. Brett's stomach cramped and the coffee felt like it boiled down deep inside him. It had always been the two of them like peas in a pod. One bright, the other dark, a perfect complement. Now they'd damaged their relationship and Brett wasn't sure it could be repaired.

Trevor smiled as he rode up. "Good morning, big brother. Got any of that coffee left?"

Brett's eyebrows shot up. "Sure thing. Pot's right over there on the fire."

Carson Foster was a blond man with gray eyes who seemed even quieter than Brett, if that was possible. He dismounted and nodded, then walked over to the coffee. Trevor stayed behind, fiddling with his mount's reins.

"I was kind of hoping you'd come to Cheyenne to see me when everyone else did."

Brett forced himself to swallow a gulp of the scalding brew. "Wasn't sure you wanted me there."

Trevor slapped his hands with the leather. "Why not? You're my brother, Brett, even if you tried to steal my woman."

Brett didn't bother to deny it. Trevor had left Adelaide when she most needed him. She was a wonderful woman, beautiful, smart, sassy. Brett had entertained the notion of courting her, but never did. He hadn't done anything wrong. Sort of.

"I didn't try to steal her." He held up a hand to forestall Trevor's mouth from running. "But I did think about it. And for that I'm sorry. You're my brother and I should have respected your feelings for her."

Trevor looked as surprised as Brett felt. He didn't know that was what he was going to say until he said it. Alex was turning him into a mushy mess.

"I accept your apology. You were invited, in fact, you're always invited." Trevor grinned and held out his hand.

Brett appeared to be possessed by unnamed forces again because he hugged Trevor. Enthusiastically. He was definitely turning soft.

As if he'd conjured her, Alex appeared just as they stepped away from each other. "All better now?"

"Alex!" Trevor picked her up and twirled her around. "It's good to see my favorite doc. How are you?"

"I was good until now. You'd better stop unless you want to have my breakfast too." She laughed until he set her down.

"You hanging around this fool brother of mine?"

She put her arm through Brett's and squeezed. "Yes, I sure am."

Brett put his hand over hers. "This one's taken."

Trevor threw back his head and laughed. "So am I."

Within an hour, the rest of the family gathered at the Square One to review the plan for saving the ranch. They surrounded him, giving him strength and courage and love. Brett had been grateful when they helped build his barn, but this...this was so much more and Brett was not only thankful but proud to be a Malloy. Kincaid was decidedly absent from the group. Whenever family gathered, he turned into a ghost.

Brett filled them in on everything that had happened the last three weeks. When he revealed the revelation that King had killed Byron, shock and anger erupted. Lots of shouting and cussing, along with disbelief.

"Why the hell did he kill Byron?"

"My guess is King tried to force Byron into making Alex marry him. He's been asking her to marry him for years," Ray offered.

"For years?" Brett had a hard time believing that.

"Yes, years. She's told me about it before."

How the hell did Ray know about King asking Alex to marry him when Brett didn't? Had he been living with blinders on that long? He'd known King had been visiting her, but he'd had no idea about King trying to get Alex to marry him. King had already had two wives, why did he want Alex? Brett felt like an idiot. A humbling moment to be sure. He didn't know what to say that wouldn't embarrass him.

"He's a persistent man," he mused.

"No, he's not persistent. He's obsessed." Ray's scowl deepened as he stared at Alex. "No man chases a woman for that long. She's told him no, hasn't ever even danced or had a meal with the man. Yet he kept pestering her. I should've had Jim talk to him."

No, Brett should have. In fact, he should have asked her to marry him twelve years ago and none of it would have happened. Too many "should haves" to count.

"Is there any evidence that King killed Byron?" his father asked. His normally open face mirrored the tension in the air.

"Some, but I'll let Jim give you those details. I don't know enough to tell right from left right now." Brett ran his hands down his face. He turned to Alex. "I'm sorry, honey. I didn't know."

She cupped his cheek. "It's okay, Brett. You have nothing to be sorry about. He's a pitiful excuse for a human being."

That was the truth if he'd ever heard it. The trick was, how to get him off their backs. While the rest of the family talked, Brett asked Carson to review the papers relating to the ranch's legal problems. The two of them found a quiet corner and sat down.

As Carson read each paper carefully, Brett itched to stand up and go for a ride, to escape. He had no idea what the lawyer would say. Carson was as much a stranger as someone he'd see on the streets of Cheyenne. However, he'd assisted Adelaide and done it honestly. Since he wasn't from Cheshire, he hoped King wouldn't be able to influence Carson's commitment to helping him.

Carson finally looked up at Brett with his unreadable gaze. "You won this ranch in a poker game, is that correct?"

"Yep, that's about the whole of it. Old Martin just threw the deed in the pot. I told him not to, but he told me he didn't have anyone to leave it to." Brett shrugged. "I never even knew he had children."

Carson glanced at the papers again. "Although you won the deed to the ranch in a poker game, the actual transfer of the deed was legal and registered with the county and is therefore valid. The man claiming to be Martin Samson's son has no legal claim on it."

Brett let out a huge sigh of relief. "Are you sure?"

"Positive." It was hard to tell what the attorney was thinking. His expression never seemed to change.

"Thank God."

"There's something else, too." Carson shuffled through the papers. "This document indicates that Martin Samson had two sons."

Brett nodded. "That's what we figured when we found the old furniture in the house."

"Where's the other son?"

"I don't know. I didn't even expect this one to show up." Brett scowled. "Does it matter where the other son is?"

"It might. I'm going to ride into town and wire a friend in Houston to check on this for me." He neatened the papers until they were precisely stacked in his hand. "Hopefully he can get back to me quickly."

"Right quick. Judge Harris is going to listen to the claim tomorrow. Can you stay until then and be my lawyer? I can't pay much but..." Brett's entire future depended on winning this case, and he wasn't above begging for help at this point.

Carson held up a hand. "Yes I will be here until tomorrow. As far as my legal fees go, they've been paid already."

Brett had a feeling he knew who had paid the legal fees and he didn't have to ask why Trevor would have arranged for it before they even spoke. Family. That's the only reason required.

The sound of rapid hoofbeats reached them.

"Brett, you here?" Slim's voice sounded from outside the barn.

Brett heard a thread of panic in his tone and hurried out to meet the old cowpoke. Slim sat atop his lathered horse, breathing as hard as the animal.

"What's going on, Slim?"

"Gunfight. Town." He coughed. "That gunslinger Ford called out your friend Kincaid. Right outta the saloon. He outright challenged him to a gunfight, but Kincaid didn't budge. Then Ford threatened you and the doc. They're supposed to fight at three o'clock."

Brett glanced at Alex, her face a mixture of fear and horror. "What time is it?"

Alex glanced at the watch pinned to her blouse. "Five after two."

That left less than an hour to get to town, a trip that normally took an hour. If they rode the hell out of the horses, maybe they'd get there in time. Kincaid was trying to save them, but Brett wouldn't allow him to sacrifice his life.

Chapter Fifteen

The August heat baked Kincaid's brain. He leaned against the wall outside the saloon and watched a lizard run beneath the wooden sidewalk. It was nearly time—ten minutes until his life ended, whether he died or not. He'd given up gunslinging for good, yet he'd been dragged back into it because of his loyalty to a friend.

Brett had turned out to be a man Kincaid not only trusted, but liked. A quiet man with pride, intelligence and commitment, he'd shown Kincaid life could be enjoyed no matter the circumstances. Malloy had been kind and giving when he didn't need to be. Kincaid would be no kind of friend if he let Ford have the doc and Brett.

Mike the bartender poked his head out and looked at Kincaid. "You want a whiskey before you start?"

Kincaid shook his head. "No, thanks. I don't need my hands to shake."

"Well if'n you win, come back in and you get one on the house."

"Thanks. I'll take you up on that in about ten more minutes."

Pretending to be a cowboy and being around good folks like the Malloys wasn't in the cards for a man like him. No one knew what Kincaid had done to survive. The dark secrets that lurked in his heart would stay there, locked away. After the gunfight, he'd either be fitted for a coffin or riding to a different town, a different life. Until that, too, soured and he had to leave.

Too bad it had to happen, but sometimes things were inevitable. Kincaid's past always caught up to him, one way or another. He couldn't outrun it or hide from it, so he might as well embrace it.

"Kincaid, what are you doing?" Sheriff Jim Weissman stepped up next to him, looking harried and more than annoyed.

"Not much."

The sheriff snorted. "That's a pile of manure. I hear tell that you are going to have a gunfight right here on the street with that lowlife King hired. That true?"

Kincaid pulled a rolled cigarette from his shirt pocket and lit it. After a drag, he blew out the smoke slowly. "What if I were?"

"I'd have to stop you. There's laws against gunfighting now, you know. You fellas can't just walk out into the streets and gun each other down because you feel like it." The sheriff put his hand on the pistol riding his thigh. "I can lock you up. Brett would probably want me to."

Kincaid knew what he was saying. The sheriff could stop the gunfight by locking him up, thereby saving his life. Kincaid didn't want that. Today was the day he was set to leave Cheshire and he didn't want the sheriff interfering.

"You could, but you won't. I haven't done anything wrong."

"But you will."

Kincaid shrugged. "Maybe. What are you going to do, follow me around like my mother?"

"No, I'll just stand right here next to you." The sheriff leaned against the post and folded his arms across his chest.

Kincaid knew the man was a friend of the Malloys, had grown up with Brett. There wasn't any way Kincaid could convince him to skedaddle.

"Your choice. I'm just standing here enjoying the heat."

A snort met his comment. "Hm, me too. I love sweating until I gotta peel my shirt off at the end of the day and my stink could kill squirrels."

Kincaid ignored him. He had to focus, to concentrate on the task ahead. His life depended on his accuracy. He closed his eyes and emptied his mind. Time to prepare.

CR800Y2

Brett rode like the hounds of hell were chasing him. He pushed Rusty as hard as he could. The roan had heart and did what was asked of him. Trevor, Ray and Noah rode behind him, keeping up with a wild man on a wild horse.

Alex would more than likely hop on Rowdy and ride into town too. She wouldn't be able to wait until he returned to know what happened. Aside from her curiosity, Alex was the town doctor and needed to be on hand for any injuries that might result.

Brett prayed they'd get there in time. It wasn't right for any man to die for a piece of property, especially when it didn't even belong to him.

When the town buildings came into view, Brett didn't dare look at the time. If three o'clock had passed, he didn't want to know. He rounded the bend by the saloon and spotted two men in the street a few blocks away.

God, he was almost too late. Brett rode his horse toward them, willing to throw himself and his horse in the middle of the gunfight. He heard someone shouting and realized Jim was being held back by King's men. King stood by watching it all like a night at the theatre.

"Kincaid, I'm warning you. Don't do it."

Brett heard the shots just as he reached them. Both gunfighters went down and Brett vaulted off the horse toward King, filled with rage. He was too late to help Kincaid. The bastard King had engineered the death of the one person in his life he could call a friend.

Brett slammed into King at full force. Fortunately he wasn't expecting it, the only advantage Brett had. The big bastard outweighed him by at least fifty pounds and was half a foot taller. Brett hit him so hard, they both tumbled backwards onto the wood-planked sidewalk.

Out of the corner of his eye, he saw Trevor and Ray take down the men holding Jim, then Brett had to focus on the Viking underneath him. The hit must have knocked the breath out of him because King didn't put up much of a fight at first. From his perch on the big man's chest, Brett punched him with a right hook, then a left jab, and finished with an uppercut.

King looked stunned and furious. He almost threw Brett off when he finally got a breath in. Brett hung on though and rode the storm of punches King threw. Then King kicked him in the back of the head and he saw stars, but he still held on.

"Little fucker, get off me!"

"I'm sick and tired of your shit. Why can't you just let folks live their lives?" Brett grabbed him by the shirtfront, staring down into King's eyes. "Why?"

King laughed. "Because I can, that's why. Life's too short to give anything away. You've got some things I want. Give them to me and I'll leave you alone."

Brett didn't believe that for a moment. He heard a gunshot, then felt a sting on his right arm as he struggled with King. A second gunshot echoed through the street. When Brett realized he'd been shot, King took advantage and threw Brett off. He landed on his back on the ground ten feet away. King seemed to have the strength of two men. Brett tried to catch his breath, but King kicked him in the side.

The toe of King's boot felt like it had a dagger in it. Pain shot through his ribs. The second kick almost made him black out. He heard signs of a struggle all around him, punches, grunts, shouts, and then finally hoofbeats.

King was so intent on killing Brett, he didn't pay attention to the horse, but Brett did. Alex, like an avenging angel on her big horse, jumped over his prone body, knocking King to the ground.

"Bastard," she hissed as she turned the horse around and aimed right for him.

King stood and faced her, as if he was impenetrable to being trampled by a horse. At the last moment, he shifted then grabbed her off the horse. She yelped and kicked out. Brett's fury exploded when he saw King holding the woman he loved like a puppy by its scruff.

Brett got to his feet, blood dripping from more than one spot on his body. "Let her go."

When King turned toward him, Brett threw the punch of his life, knocking King to the ground. Brett's hand felt like it had been stepped on by a horse, but he ignored it. Alex fell beside him, then rolled away. She was on her feet in seconds. King lay between them, unmoving.

"Did I kill him?"

"I don't think so, but you knocked him unconscious." She smiled until she saw his face. "Dear God."

"I'm fine, honey. Don't worry about me. Check on Kincaid."

Alex kissed him quickly then ran toward the gunslinger who lay in the street. Brett stared down at King, wondering what would make someone so selfish and greedy as to try to destroy other people's lives for their own gain. Jim walked up beside them, limping, a bevy of bruises and cuts on his face and fists.

"That big son of a bitch is going in my jail and his gunfighter is dead." He glanced at Brett. "You okay?"

"Not yet, but I'm better. Take care of that stupid bastard, would you?"

Jim nodded and Brett turned to see how his friend had fared. He almost didn't want to walk over to the man in black, but forced himself to move. Alex and Noah hovered over him and had bandages pressed to his side, which meant Kincaid wasn't dead. Thank God.

Brett knelt by Kincaid. His friend had glassy eyes and was as pale as milk. "You look like shit."

"Obviously." He tried to laugh but it sounded more like a sob.

"There was no reason for you to fight this battle for me." Brett touched Kincaid's shoulder. "I don't want you to die for my ranch."

"I didn't have anything worth dying for before."

Brett shook his head. "Never took you for a fool, Kincaid."

"Too bad. I knew you were a fool the moment I met the doc. Any other man would have snatched her up years ago." He glanced up at the blonde woman struggling to save his life.

"You've got that right. I was an idiot, but no more. She already saved my life today, maybe she'll save your sorry hide too."

"If I'm lucky." Kincaid grimaced in pain. Brett stayed beside him, lending whatever strength he could.

Alex looked up at him. "I've got the bleeding under control for now, but we need to get him to the clinic so I can repair the damage." She had blood smeared on her cheek, her hair blew in the breeze, and dirt all over her clothes. Brett had never loved her more.

He stood and found Ray and Trevor behind him. Without being asked, they helped Brett and Noah carry Kincaid down to the Brighton's house. Kincaid passed out within two minutes, which could be good or bad.

Alex ran ahead of them, hands busy twisting her unbound hair into a knot out of the way. She unlocked the front door and left it open, hurrying inside to prepare.

They brought Kincaid to the examining room, laying the unconscious man down as gently as they could. He groaned and his eyes fluttered open.

"Don't kick me anymore."

"I'm not kicking you, you idiot. Ford shot you." Brett removed the gunslinger's boots, noticing the man had holes in his socks.

"Did I shoot him?"

"Yes, but it doesn't matter." Brett hadn't even bothered looking at the piece of shit. "Alex is gonna fix you up."

Alex ran in with a pile of clean bandages. "There's water heating on the stove. Trevor, can you go mind it?"

Trevor nodded and was off. Brett embraced the notion his family had again stood by his side and helped him when he most needed it.

Ray shifted his feet. "I'm going to go check with Jim to see if he needs any help." Never good with healing, Ray was better off doing things he was comfortable with, like helping the sheriff.

"Thanks, Ray."

"I'll be back in a little bit to check on you." He looked at Alex. "Do you need anything from Goodson's?"

"No, thank you. I have all I need here." Alex cut away Kincaid's shirt, revealing a wad of bloody bandages.

Ray was gone before Brett could register he'd moved. Noah stood by, waiting to assist. He'd always had a healing touch with humans and animals. In fact, he served as the everyday healer at his parents' ranch.

Brett felt helpless watching Alex and Noah work, but he stayed beside his friend. Praying was about all he could do.

CRROED

Many hours and pots of coffee later, Brett sat alone in the parlor. Trevor poked his head in.

"You still here? You know it's tomorrow already."

Brett closed his eyes. "Alex finished around suppertime, but Kincaid has been unconscious since then. She needed some sleep so I told her I'd sit up and keep checking on him."

Trevor came in and sat on the chair next to the settee. He leaned forward with his elbows resting on his knees. "You surprised me."

"How so?"

He pursed his lips and stared at the floor for a few moments. "You know you're my brother and I love you, but you're a difficult man sometimes. Very quiet, too quiet really. You never talked to any of us."

"Sorry about that. I just like to keep my thoughts to myself I guess." Brett squirmed under his brother's honesty. It was all true, of course.

"I know and it took me a long while to figure that out. Then when all of that stuff happened with Adelaide..." He trailed off and took a deep breath. "I had a hard time believing you would just leave without even talking to me. It hurt."

Brett felt the pricks of a guilty conscience eat at him. "I was hurt too, Trevor. I took care of her for you, nothing more. Made sure she was safe and healthy while you went off and hunted the man who tried to kill her. You didn't trust me."

Saying it out loud hurt like a bandage being ripped off an open wound. Once done, it felt better, but it stung like a bitch.

Trevor hung his head. "No, I didn't trust *me*. You see, Adelaide made me forget every other woman. Something that's never happened before. I panicked and...I lost my head completely. I wanted to believe she would leave me as soon as I was out of sight, that way I didn't have to acknowledge I loved her." He looked up at Brett. "I know now that I acted like a complete ass and I'm sorry that I hurt you."

Brett swallowed the huge lump that had formed in his throat. "It's, ah, okay. I think there were spears thrown from both sides. Can we consider this feud over?"

"Over and done." Trevor held out his hand and Brett shook it.

"Nope, ain't gonna do it." With a laugh, they both stood and embraced.

"One more thing. Okay two more," Trevor said after they both sat back down. "Why the hell didn't you tell me about the ranch and how did you and Kincaid end up as friends?"

"Oh, the ranch." Brett took a big gulp of coffee. "I didn't tell anyone about it, not just you. It was the first thing I had that was mine and I guess I just wanted to keep it that way, until I was ready to take it over. Then I found out it was the biggest place for rats to mate."

Trevor snorted and slapped his knee. "Sounds fragrant."

"It was, believe me. I never saw so much mouse shit in my life."

"Fertilizer." Trevor grinned. "What about Kincaid?"

Brett tried to explain it. "He and I are alike. Somehow, deep down, we're of the same cloth, don't know how the hell that happened, but it did. I kind of...found a friendship I didn't know I'd been missing."

Trevor clapped him on the shoulder. "Well I hope he makes it okay. Is there anything I can do for you?"

"Just keep an eye on the herd. With King in jail, I don't think anything will happen, but I'd feel better knowing you, Ray and Noah were watching for me." Brett still didn't like asking for help, but it got easier each time.

"No problem. I'm on my way there now. Good luck."

With another handshake, Trevor left Brett alone in the parlor for a long night.

He paced and tried to read, then paced some more. Each time he peeked in at Kincaid, the other man slept on. Around three in the morning, Brett made another pot of coffee. He poured himself a nice healthy mugful, then went to the examining room to check on his friend.

"Damn, that coffee smells good. You're going to share, right?"

Brett almost dropped the cup on his foot. Kincaid's eyes were wide open and clear. In fact, he was sitting up looking as if he hadn't been shot twelve hours earlier.

"You're awake."

"Yep, I noticed that. So, what about the coffee?"

Brett stepped into the room and handed the mug to Kincaid. He took it with trembling hands and cupped the hot brew. Leaning over the mug, he took a sniff.

"I think I feel better just smelling this elixir of the gods. Thanks, Brett." Kincaid took a tentative sip, then a gulp. "Ahhh."

"I thought you were going to die," Brett blurted.

Kincaid arched one dark eyebrow. "I did."

That didn't make any sense at all. He figured Kincaid had something to say so he didn't respond. Usually silence made people jabber on, one of Brett's most effective weapons against his brothers growing up.

"You see I figured, no matter what happened I'd die on that street. I tried"—he swallowed hard—"I tried to make a life without using my guns, but they jumped into my hands again."

Brett sat on the edge of the examining table. "So, are you saying you want to be dead?"

Kincaid sighed. "No, but I have to be. No matter if I try to run from it, my past will catch me sooner or later." He glanced at Brett. "I can't let anyone else get hurt because of it."

"That's a load of shit. I wasn't hurt and neither was Alex."

"But you almost were. I saw your idiot ass ride in and then Alex. Foolhardy woman. Thought she was a goner for sure." He shook his head. "Don't you see, killing follows me sure as a dog follows his nose."

Brett understood what Kincaid was trying to say. He'd spent so long being a gunslinger that his life revolved around it. Any step to the left or right brought the gunslinging right back to him. What a crushing blow to accept.

"I hope you're wrong."

"But you know I'm not."

Brett nodded. "You know you're always welcome at the Square One, no matter what you decide. I know I speak for me, Alex and Mason when I say we'd like you to stay."

Kincaid cleared his throat and swallowed a huge gulp of the coffee. He wheezed and held his side as the hot brew slid into him. "Shit that's hot."

"Thus the entire purpose of hot coffee."

Kincaid chuckled rustily. "And you say you're not funny."

"I'm not trying to be funny. I was just telling the truth."

With a grin, Kincaid took another, smaller mouthful of coffee. "I'm going to miss the ranch."

"We'll miss you too. Guess there's no chance you'll stay right?" Brett hoped Kincaid would change his mind, but he knew his friend wouldn't. It wasn't a simple decision, and it couldn't be changed easily.

"Nope. I probably won't say goodbye either. Just keep my horse at the livery for me and I'll leave when I'm able." A flash of ancient pain passed through his dark eyes. "Thank you for everything, Brett. Strange as it may seem, I think you're the first man I call friend."

"Not strange at all." Brett fought against the damn lump forming in his throat. "I know exactly what you mean."

They sat together and talked for another half an hour until Kincaid's eyelids drooped. Brett took the mug and made sure he was covered, then said goodbye to his friend as silently as the night around him.

The sun arrived full of summer heat. After a restless night, Alex found Brett sleeping on the settee in the parlor. His neck was bent at an awkward angle. It hurt her just to look at him. She leaned down and kissed him. He awoke in an instant, startled and frantic.

"Jesus Christ! Is everything okay? What's going on?"

"Yes, everything is okay. I'm sorry, I didn't mean to scare you." She hid a grin behind her hand. His hair looked like he'd been pulling at it for hours and the whiskers lent him an air of sexiness.

"It's okay." He rubbed his hand down his face. "How is he?"

"He's fine. Resting comfortably. Kincaid insists he's leaving in the next two days. Stubborn idiot." She touched the cut above his eye and the bruise on his jaw. "You should have let me doctor you."

"You did."

"One bullet graze doesn't count." She frowned. "You've got some cuts here that might need stitches."

Brett scowled. "I don't need any more stitches, thank you very much."

She laughed and kissed him again. "That lawyer Carson was at the door a few minutes ago. Said your case was being heard in an hour."

Brett looked like a deer in a hunter's sights. "Oh my God. I forgot about the case. Hell, I look like shit and I smell pretty bad too. That's not going to win any case for me."

He struggled to stand and Alex touched his arm.

"It's okay, sweetheart. Carson went to go have breakfast. You can shave with my father's razor and Trevor brought by clothes for you."

Brett let out a breath. "Thank God for family. Okay, let me get cleaned up and I'll go find that Carson fella."

He stood and started to walk out of the room, then stopped and came back. Brett cupped her face in his large hands and kissed her breathless.

"Thank you, Alex, for everything. For saving my life, for saving Kincaid and for loving me."

Alex stood there like an idiot for several minutes while her lips tingled and her heart beat a steady tattoo. God, she loved that man.

CB⬥BD

Brett stood outside the meeting hall and pulled at his collar. Sweat dripped down his back from the heat and the fear that weighed heavily on him. Just the thought of losing everything to the drunk son of a bitch who stood nearby made him sick to his stomach. Tim Green stood beside Parker, avoiding Brett's gaze. He should. The lousy bastard had sold his soul to a devil named King.

Parker Samson was barely conscious and looked as if he'd spent the night swimming in a vat of whiskey. He smelled, he was dirty, and his eyes kept closing. God knows when the man last bathed.

Brett felt a smidge better about his own appearance, but not much. He'd shaved, but almost cut his own throat because his hand shook. His hair was combed and his face clean, and at least his clothes were presentable.

Carson stood beside him, papers in hand, not a drop of sweat in sight. It had to be nearly eighty degrees already and the dapper man looked like he was in a drawing room instead of a dusty street in Wyoming.

"I heard from my colleague in Houston." Carson spoke to Brett quietly. "He found the information we needed."

Brett's eyes widened. "What did he find?"

"Apparently—"

A young man with slicked-back hair poked his head out the door. "The judge is ready for you now."

Whatever Carson was going to say had to wait. He was a smart man, and Brett had confidence that whatever he found would only help his case.

The two men and their attorneys marched into the meeting hall. Judge Harris was a stern-looking man with silver hair and dark eyes. He sat behind a desk so Brett could not tell his height, but he intimidated the hell out of him anyway.

Four ladder back chairs sat in front of him.

"Sit." Judge Harris gestured to the chairs and the four of them sat. Or rather, three of them sat. Parker fell into his chair. The judge frowned at him. "Are you all right, young man?"

"Just fine." Parker let loose a belch.

The judge quirked one eyebrow but didn't say anything else to him. "This case in front of me today is one Parker Samson versus Brett Malloy. Are both parties and their attorneys present?"

"Yes, your Honor," Carson answered. "Carson Fuller for Brett Malloy."

"T-Tim Green for Parker Samson." The lawyer's glance skittered across Brett. Too bad he had nothing to throw at the son of a bitch.

"I've reviewed the claim by Mr. Samson on the property in question. Does anyone have any additional evidence to introduce?"

"Yes, I do, Your Honor." Carson stood. "I have researched the progeny of Martin Samson with the assistance of the Attorney General in Houston."

A friend? Carson was friends with the Attorney General? Brett had to admit he was impressed.

"Go on." The judge gestured with his hand.

"Apparently Martin and Bernice Samson had two sons. Parker Samson died when he was ten years old, and the other, Dwayne Samson was disowned twenty years ago." Carson held up two pieces of paper. "I have Parker's death certificate and Martin Samson's will disowning Dwayne. I also have information that one Dwayne Samson is wanted in three counties in Texas for fraud. My assumption is, Your Honor, that Dwayne is using his brother's identity to avoid jail."

Parker, or more than likely Dwayne, sat up straight and swallowed hard. "That's a lie. I ain't disowned. I mean, I ain't dead."

Tim Green shushed him.

"Hand that up here, young man."

Carson brought the papers to the judge and returned to Brett with a small ghost of a smile on his face.

After scanning the documents, the judge glanced up at them. "Does anyone else want to speak before I pass judgment?"

Carson glanced at Brett. "Would you like to speak?"

Brett's tongue froze right along with his brain. Him, speak?

"It's your property, so it's your choice," Carson offered.

Brett swallowed and glanced at the judge. The intimidating expression hadn't changed. In fact, he looked even more annoyed than before.

"Yes, I'd like to say something."

"Well, get on with it then, I've got another case to hear today and I've got to get over to Hawk's Bend before noon." Judge Harris straightened the papers in front of him.

Brett stood. "I, um, never expected to have my own ranch, sir. When I won it from old Martin, I mean, Martin Samson, I tried to give it back. He asked me to take care of it after he was gone. I gave him my word I would." He took a breath. "I've kept my word and put my heart and soul into that ranch. Fixed up the house and the barn, even put a herd on the property. I've lived here in Cheshire all my life and I'll be proud to raise my children here. Uh, thank you."

The judge glanced at Tim, who fidgeted in his seat. "Anything for Mr. Samson? Parker or Dwayne?"

Parker jerked and looked like a scared rabbit. "I ain't got nothing to say."

Tim cleared his throat. "Parker is the rightful heir to Martin Samson's property, therefore the ranch should be his."

"That about it?" The judge speared Tim with his sharp gaze.

"Y-yes, sir."

"Hmph, okay then. I'm ready to pass judgment on this case." He pointed his finger at Brett. "I find for Mr. Malloy. Case closed."

Brett sat there staring at the older man while Carson stood and started to walk away. Jim appeared and took Parker's arm with a grin.

"I've got a cell with your name on it, Samson."

Parker whined while Tim ran like a rat deserting a sinking ship.

"Brett?" Carson looked back at him.

"Mr. Malloy, is there anything else?" Judge Harris frowned.

"Just wanted to say thank you."

"No need to thank me. It was a legal judgment, not a personal one."

"That doesn't matter to me. I say thank you when folks do me a kindness, even if it's a legal one. So, thank you." He stuck out his trembling hand and the judge shook it.

"You're welcome, young man. Make sure you work that ranch well."

Brett smiled. "I plan on it."

Brett walked out of the meeting hall feeling a thousand pounds lighter. Carson waited for him outside.

"I'm glad it all worked out, Brett. I'm going to head back to Cheyenne today."

"Thank you for everything, Carson. If I can ever return the favor, you just holler." Brett shook the other man's hand.

Carson inclined his head and walked toward his waiting mount. That's when Brett saw Alex. She stood beside Rusty with anxiety written all over her pretty face. He ran toward her and scooped her up into his arms.

"I won. The ranch is ours, honey. All ours."

She squealed and hung onto his neck, raining kisses all over his face. "Oh, Brett, I'm so happy for you."

"Ahem, you two want to stop that?" Trevor said from behind them. "Makes me miss my Adelaide something fierce. You probably don't want to see me when I'm missing my woman."

Brett laughed and set Alex on her feet. "How's Kincaid?"

"He's fine. Margaret came in to spell me so I could be here." She touched his cheek. "Jim came by and told me King is being charged with Papa's murder." Tears stood in her eyes.

"Good. I'm glad to hear he'll pay for killing at least one person. No doubt he's done it before." Brett looked at Trevor. "Will you ride back to the Square One with me before you leave?"

"Of course. I've got something to show you anyway." Trevor winked at Alex and she chuckled.

"What are you two up to?"

"Nothing. Not a thing. No sirree, not a thing." Trevor whistled as he mounted Silver. "Coming, big brother?"

With an annoyed grunt, Brett helped Alex onto Rowdy then mounted his own horse. The three of them rode out to the Square One together. Everything looked normal. Except Mason.

The boy was clean, really clean. Not just quick wash with soap, but squeaky clean with new clothes too. He stood next to the corral grinning. Ray leaned on the post, arms folded across his chest.

"About time you got back to your ranch," Ray groused. "I was about to grow cobwebs waiting on you."

"What are you talking about? I was in t—"

The words flew from his mouth when he saw the bull. A big, beautiful bull roaming the pasture behind the barn, safely behind a brand-new fence. His heart nearly stopped.

"Is that my bull?"

"Yes, it surely is. I kept it over at my place until this morning." Ray smiled. "Trevor brought it with him from Cheyenne from a rancher named Asa Keenan. Kincaid wanted it to be a surprise."

"That's an understatement. It's...it's wonderful." Brett's breath hitched as he struggled to absorb all the good news he'd had. It was almost too much until Alex touched him. She slid her hand into his and leaned her head on his shoulder.

"He's a beauty. What will you call him?"

"Martin. I'm going to call him Martin." And with a little luck, Martin would make the Square One a thriving ranch. Everything was coming together.

"One more surprise for you in the house. Don't blame me. It was all Mama's doing." Ray shook his hand. "I'm gonna head back home."

Brett told himself those were not tears in his eyes. "Thanks, Ray. For everything."

"Anytime, brother. Anytime."

After Ray rode away, Trevor and Mason disappeared into the barn. Alex linked her arm through his.

"Shall we look in the house?" She grinned.

"Might as well get it over with. God knows what Mama did in there."

They walked in together and Brett stopped dead in his tracks. Furniture, curtains, even a damn rug by the fireplace. A table and chairs, one he recognized from Ray's house, a couch from his parents' house, and a cushioned chair that used to

233

belong to his grandparents. Sitting on the back of the couch, a new sign for the ranch, freshly made with Brett's name. His throat tightened.

"Where did all this come from?" Alex glanced around.

"My family. Looks like things they haven't been using or didn't need." Brett's heart couldn't get much fuller.

"Should we check out the bedroom?" Alex waggled her eyebrows.

Brett closed the front door with a grin. "By all means."

They walked into the bedroom to find a beautifully made bed, covered with a wedding ring quilt Brett didn't recognize. More than likely his mother and her friends had been busy sewing since he'd told her about asking Alex to marry him.

The quilt had varying shades of green, brown and blue. A vase of flowers sat on a small table beside the bed, a mixture of buds that grew wild. They filled the room with their beautiful scent.

"It even smells good in here."

Brett shut the door behind them and wrapped his arms around Alex. He buried his nose in her neck. "Not as good as you."

He kissed the side of her neck and ear, absorbing all that was Alex. He smelled her arousal as it rose as quickly as his did. His heart was full to bursting. He'd never expected life would give him so much. The ranch, his family, a good friend and Alex. She was everything.

Brett remembered standing in this room after Jack had brought the beautiful furniture he'd made. He had wanted Alex there, and here she was, soft and warm in his arms. Soon they'd be married and every morning and every night they'd begin and end their days together in this room. Their private sanctuary against the world.

Here he felt safe. He felt loved.

He leaned down and pressed his lips against her ear and whispered, "I love you."

After a short intake of breath, she whispered, "I love you, too."

Brett turned her around and looked into her beautiful, brown eyes and saw his heart reflected back. She smiled and he knew everything would be all right.

They undressed each other. Each button brought a kiss to the exposed skin. With the ease of two lovers who knew each others' bodies, Brett and Alex caressed, teased and kissed until they lay naked on the new wedding quilt that adorned their soon-to-be marriage bed.

Alex ran her hands through his hair. "Should we be doing this on the wedding quilt?"

Brett pressed his mouth to hers and gave her a long, delicious kiss. When he pulled back, all humor had fled from her face. She looked like a woman in love, in lust, a woman who was all his. As he was hers.

"Yes, we should. Even though we haven't said the words with a preacher, you're my wife, and I love you."

A sheen of tears filled her eyes. "I love you too, Brett. You take my breath away."

As his mouth descended again, he shut out the rest of the world. He didn't hear anything but her breathing and the beat of her heart. He kissed his way across her jaw to her neck while cupping her breast. He rolled the nipple between his thumb and forefinger, tweaking and teasing. He sucked her neck, a gentle bite, a lick, a kiss.

Alex caressed his back, landing on his buttocks, squeezing. She moved closer, pressing his hardened flesh against her softness. Heaven, sweet, sweet heaven.

"God you feel good," he groaned.

"I could say the same thing about you."

Before he knew it, he was flat on his back and she was above him. Her unbound hair brushed against his skin like a lover's caress. He shivered in anticipation of what she'd do. After a quick hard kiss to the lips, Alex proceeded to kiss, lick and bite her way down his body, sending him into an arousal so strong blood rushed past his ears.

Her tongue circled his bellybutton while her long-fingered hands stroked his inner thighs. Brett had an idea of what she was going to do and he about spilled his seed at the thought of it. She placed kisses all around his needy flesh and then her mouth finally closed around the head of his cock. He hissed in pleasure as heat ricocheted through him.

"Oh, God, Alex, oh God."

She licked him from bottom to top then closed her hand around the breadth of him.

"God surely did bless you, Brett. Perhaps I should say He blessed me."

Brett tried to chuckle but he found himself strangely paralyzed by her touch. Her pink lips opened and she took him into the hot, wet recess of her mouth, and he couldn't think anymore.

Her tongue, her lips, her teeth. She pleasured him with her mouth. It could have been two minutes; it could have been two hundred. He didn't know. Time had no meaning. The sensations were amazing, shattering. If he wasn't careful, her sweet ministrations would end his pleasure before she had hers.

As much as it pained him to do so, the next time she pulled him out of her mouth, he put a hand on her shoulder to stop her. He wouldn't be able to hold back any longer. The blood rushed around his body, leaving tingles in its wake. He'd never been so aroused or so pleasured in his life.

"I need to be inside you, Alex. Please."

She glanced down at his cock glistening with the moisture from her tongue.

"One more taste." When she licked it one last time from top to bottom and squeezed his balls, Brett grabbed the sheets to keep from coming his brains out.

With a grin she must have borrowed from Eve, Alex moved up and positioned herself over him. Inch by inch, he sank into her tight core. The throbbing in her pussy matched the pulse in his cock. Fast, hard, furious with need.

The torture continued when she slid up and down slowly, nearly taking him out of her body before she descended again. Brett couldn't handle the pace anymore.

With a flip, she was beneath him, her legs spread wide, Brett's cock firmly nestled inside her. She smiled and licked her lips.

"Did it feel good?"

"Oh, honey." He leaned down and bit both of her nipples. "You have no idea."

She tightened around him, arching her back to offer up her breasts like a feast. Brett pleasured her while he thrust inside her, again and again. The frenzy of their joining seemed more like a mating, a branding of two souls, two hearts.

He reached between them and flicked her hot button as his ecstasy reached its peak. Alex screamed his name and her legs closed around his hips, milking him, pulling him in deeper.

The orgasm hit him so hard, his heart stuttered and his vision blurred. Wave after wave of the purest of pleasure crashed over him. He held onto her, riding the storm until the tremors passed.

Breathing hard, he rolled off her and lay beside her, hands entwined.

"I guess we christened this quilt."

Alex laughed and squeezed his hand. "You really are very funny, Brett Malloy."

"I wasn't being funny." He smiled at her and waggled his eyebrows. "I was only telling the truth."

With one last kiss, Alex tucked herself under his chin and snuggled beside him. Brett's heart danced with joy at what he held in his arms.

Life, it seemed, had finally begun.

About the Author

You can't say cowboys without thinking of Beth Williamson. She likes 'em hard, tall and packing. Read her work and discover for yourself how hot and dangerous a cowboy can be.

Beth lives in North Carolina, with her husband and two sons. Born and raised in New York, she holds a B.F.A. in writing from New York University. She spends her days as a technical writer, and her nights immersed in writing hot romances for her readers.

To learn more about Beth Williamson, please visit www.bethwilliamson.com. Send an email to Beth at beth@bethwilliamson.com, join her Yahoo! Group, http://groups.yahoo.com/group/cowboylovers, or sign up for Beth's monthly newsletter, Sexy Spurs, http://www.crocodesigns.com/cgi-bin/dada/mail.cgi/list/spurs/

Look for these titles

Now Available

The Bounty
The Prize
The Reward
The Treasure
The Gift
The Tribute

Coming Soon:

The Legacy
Marielle's Marshall
Devils on Horseback: Nate
Branded

She's a princess desperate for a husband. He's a duke...or is he?

A Beautiful Surrender
© 2007 Brenda Williamson

With her uncle poised to steal her kingdom, Princess Katerina must marry. Miraculously, a new handsome duke appears on the scene. His sexy charm makes her tingle from head to toe. But can she overlook his arrogance?

The future of Dax's country is at stake. Forced to masquerade as a duke to seduce Katerina and prevent her from marrying, he courts the princess with great success. But when someone tries to kill Katerina, his instincts are to protect the passionate lady no matter the cost.

With Dax's deception revealed and her life at risk, can Katerina still surrender her heart?

Available now in ebook and print from Samhain Publishing.

Enjoy the following excerpt from A Beautiful Surrender…

Dax hadn't expected the princess to be beautiful. He knew nothing of Katerina when he came to Alluvia and beyond her appearance, she had an inner quality he found appealing—loneliness. He identified it well from experience. She wanted someone to cherish her for herself and not for her position or wealth. That awareness made him feel off balance dealing with her, because he wanted the very same for himself.

"Was your journey here uneventful, Your Grace?" the princess asked, not responding to his bid for a more personal acquaintance.

"Won't you even try to call me Dax?" He slipped his arm around her back and drew her against him as if they were going to dance on the sidelines of the ballroom.

"I'm sorry, Your Grace, but it would not be proper for me to address you so informally, nor is it appropriate for you to hold me this close."

He waltzed her along slower than everyone else danced, steering her farther from the view of her brother.

"Proper and appropriate are what you make of it, Princess. You appear capable of deciding for yourself what is suitable." He gave in to decorum and danced her into the crowd on the ballroom floor. "Unless you're…never mind."

The princess's soft brown eyes looked up at him with greater interest than he expected. All his information about Princess Katerina of Alluvia had, of course, been tainted by the source. She could hardly be considered a shrew or cold-hearted. Not when she gazed at him with the lustful passion of a woman willing to compromise her reputation. She spoke of them being too close, but not once did she try to remove herself from his embrace.

"Or what?" Her sweet breath fanned his face.

"Or, Your Highness, might I suggest you are uncomfortable in a man's arms?" he teased.

"I've danced in the arms of many men and I see no threat to be in yours."

"And your heart?" He pressed his hand to her back, forcing her to feel the pounding of his heart upon her breasts and discovering hers rapidly beating, too.

"What does my heart have to do with dancing?" Her eyes grew curious with a delightful sparkle, as if she were an innocent child.

"Does it always beat this fast and hard, as if trapped in a cage?"

The princess shook her head violently in several short turns. Two curls sprung free and bobbed over her left eye. Her silent protest spoke the opposite of what she wanted him to think and know about her.

Dax put a hand up and tucked the curls back into the arranged swirls. He didn't tell her how soft and silky the strands were—his attraction grew strong, like she possessed the magic to put him under a spell. He enjoyed the sensation of happiness, but now was not the right time to forget he worked toward destroying her to save his kingdom.

Wherever they went, the sea of people parted like two waves. Dax and Katerina moved carelessly between the wakes. The brightly lit room concealed nothing about the woman. She carried herself as regally as any noble. Her willowy figure intrigued him enough that he overstepped boundaries, sliding his hands wherever he pleased.

On the small of her back, he felt the heat of her body. Endowed with a healthy set of breasts on her sleek, streamlined frame, the way the princess had them cinched up in her clothing appeared to be uncomfortable. Taking note of the soft ivory swells made his cock stiff and his erection battle the cloth.

"Might I suggest some refreshments?" Dax didn't wait for her answer. He needed a drink and a reprieve from her delicious, warm body rubbing his.

From a servant passing by, he plucked two long-stemmed crystal flutes from a tray. Handing one to the princess, he took a swig from the other. Over the rim of the glass, he watched Katerina's mouth part. The fine crystal touched her dusky bottom lip and she tipped the glass, gingerly sipping the wine. Her tongue peeked out and ran a slow trail over her top lip. The elegant drama enchanting him didn't end when she took another sip and the bubbles tickled her nose. She lifted a hand immediately to ward off a sneeze she didn't get to stop.

Dax put a hand to hers, holding the glass to prevent her from spilling the drink. He looked deep into her wonderful stare. A hundred places to kiss her and he thought of nowhere else than the tip of her nose. At the first chance he got, he would.

The princess shivered.

"Are you cold?" He continued holding her hand on the glass stem.

"Actually, I'm quite hot."

Her warm, wine-flavored breath caught his and tugged encouragingly at his lips. With little effort on his part, he could have her against him. From toes to nose, he wanted to meld their flesh with the thrill of passion.

"That doesn't seem hard to imagine with all the people in this room generating body heat." He envisioned his tongue thrusting between her slightly parted, plum-tinted lips, tasting the wine the way she had.

Dax discarded his fluted crystal on the credenza next to him. Then, right as her eyes blinked, he put a hand on her hip and one between her shoulder blades. The princess slid her foot closer. Her thigh brushed his and her breasts pressed against his chest. The pearlescent skin rose above the edge of her violet gown. He recognized her perfume as an infusion of rose petal water—a scent he never appreciated until now. Something else had been added. After another deep inhale, he suspected it was the natural fragrance of her sex.

Katerina's hips shifted and he moved his leg, accommodating her fit and sensing a preclimactic tension. He forced his knee against her gown, into the juncture of her thighs. She took a deeper breath. Her glassy gaze held a blend of trepidation and confusion. His stance blocked her from public view. Though not enough to prevent a passerby from seeing their closeness—tightening, aligning and fitting together as only lovers should.

The tragedy of Katerina letting the duke kiss her would be, she'd love it. She'd adore the moment, the man and the sensations of being a woman. Then he'd abandon her. She didn't know much about men, even with her brother's antics giving her insight as to what they were like. He showed sweet devotion to one and then another without ever realizing the consequences to the woman.

Katerina looked into the devil's blue eyes. Each time his fingers moved, she repositioned. Every time his body twisted, she turned to fit. The pores in her skin dampened and she shivered again. Expectation and desire held her back from the boldness of begging him to kiss her.

"We're too close."

"I know." He had his hands in all the wrong places for public appearance.

"You should move away."

"Or you could."

She looked at his naturally tanned skin and the hint of whiskers peppering his jaw. His eyebrows were combed flat and his teeth resembled polished chips of white marble. Only someone so near might notice the hair in his nose was clipped. Yet, she didn't want anyone else to be as she was, where his lips might touch hers or their lashes fold together. Fantasies rose high in her mind. For once she didn't force them away.

The duke's hand squeezed her bottom and she heard an embarrassing moan escape her throat. As if testing her voice, he kneaded the quivering cheek of her ass again, pulling and forcing her tighter into his crotch.

His other hand slipped up her back. Scorching fingers folded around the nape of her neck and held her head firmly. She couldn't begin to think where she should put her hands.

"If I don't move, what will you do?" Her body went through a series of titillating sensations in response to the heat between them.

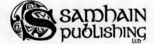